The Brave Toy Soldier

...and other stories

Published in 2015 by Bounty Books,
a division of Octopus Publishing Group Ltd,
Carmelite House
50 Victoria Embankment,
London EC4Y 0DZ
www.octopusbooks.co.uk

An Hachette UK Company
www.hachette.co.uk

Illustrated by Maureen Bradley.

ISBN: 978-0-75373-051-5

A CIP catalogue record for this book is available from the British Library.

Printed and bound by CPI Group (UK) Ltd, Croydon, CR0 4YY

CONTENTS

The Brave Toy Soldier

There was once a toy soldier who lived in Gerry's toybox. He was very big, as big as a doll, and he was made of wood. He wore a black busby, a red coat, blue trousers, and carried a fine sword.

One day a dreadful thing happened to him. Gerry threw all his toys out of the toybox on to the floor, and the soldier rolled on to the hearthrug. When Gerry put the toys back, he didn't notice the wooden soldier on the rug. He left him there – and that evening when his mother went to the fire to put coal on, she trod on him.

Crack! Something broke! Poor toy soldier. One of his legs broke right off, and there he was with only one leg left!

"My word!" said Mother, and she picked him up. "Whatever will Gerry say?

He will be upset! I must tell him how sorry I am tomorrow."

So she told Gerry and showed him the broken soldier. He was sorry and bound up the hurt leg in a handkerchief. Then he wanted to use the handkerchief and took it off again. The soldier was thrown into the back of the cupboard and stayed there.

When the time came for all the toys to wake up at night and play together on the floor the soldier was very unhappy. He couldn't march any more. He could only hop on his one good leg. The other leg was quite gone, for Mother had thrown it into the dustbin.

The toys were sorry for him. They crowded round him and helped him to hop.

"I'm not a bit of use now," said the toy soldier, sadly. "I can't run at an enemy. I can only hop slowly along."

Now the next day a little friend came to tea with Gerry and saw the broken toy soldier. She picked it up and looked at it.

"What a horrid old toy soldier," she said. "His leg is broken. He's no more use. I will throw him out of the window. That is what I do to my broken toys."

"No, don't," said Gerry, who was very fond of his toys, even broken ones. But it was too late – the little girl had thrown the soldier out of the window and he landed with a bump on to a flower-bed below.

He lay there, too surprised to move. Then he wondered if perhaps his other leg had been broken in the fall, so he sat up and looked. What a good thing! He wasn't

hurt at all, for the flower-bed was nice and soft.

He lay there till night came, for Mother would not let Gerry go and look for him because it was raining hard. Oh dear me! The rain soaked into his red coat and blue trousers and soon all the colours ran into one another, and the poor soldier looked a perfect fright. He was horrified to see himself.

"Whatever shall I do now?" he thought. "I have lost my right leg – and all my colours have run. I am an unlucky toy!"

He got up on his one leg and hopped over the bed to the path. He didn't know what to do. He couldn't get back into the house, that was certain.

He went down the path, hoppity-hop, hoppity-hop. The moon came out and shone brightly on the poor toy soldier. On he went and came to the hedge at the bottom of the garden. He slipped through it, hoppity-hop. He came out into a field, and went along the path there.

Suddenly he stopped. He thought he could hear a little cry: "Help! Help!"

The soldier clutched his sword firmly,

and turned himself about. Someone was in trouble!

"Help! Help!" The soldier heard the cry again. He thought it came from under the hedge and he hurried there.

He heard the sound of crying as he went, and saw in the moonlight a small fairy being carried in the arms of a large and ugly goblin.

"Stop!" cried the toy soldier, and he hopped in front of the surprised goblin. He waved his sword and shouted as loudly as he could.

"What are *you*?" said the goblin,

looking the wooden soldier up and down. "Do you suppose you can stop me?"

"Yes, I do!" said the soldier and swept his sword downwards to wound the goblin. But, quick as a wink, the ugly little creature jumped aside. The soldier hopped after him, hoppity-hop.

"Ho ho!" cried the goblin, when he saw that the toy soldier had only one leg. "Ho ho! So you think you can save this fairy, do you? Well, you can't, old hop-about! I'll take you prisoner too! Ho, goblins, come and get this little wooden man!"

Up ran two more goblins and took the toy soldier between them. "Bring him

along too," commanded the first goblin. So off they all went under the hedge, the fairy carried by the first goblin, and the soldier struggling between the other two.

They went down a trapdoor and into a long passage. They came to a door and the first goblin pushed it open. It led into a large cave, the goblin's home. He set down the crying fairy on a chair, and told the other goblins to go. He slammed the door and grinned at his two prisoners.

"Now," he said to the fairy. "You will just stay here as a prisoner until you tell me all the magic you know. And you, soldier, shall be my servant and cook my meals and clean my room! That will serve you right for trying to interfere with me! Take that broom and start sweeping. As for you, fairy, just begin thinking of all the spells you know, and be ready to tell me them by the time I come back."

He went out and they heard him locking and bolting the door. There was no window, so the two were prisoners. The soldier stared at the fairy in dismay.

"I am so sorry I couldn't save you," he said. "You see, I have only one leg, and it is so difficult to do anything when I have to hop."

"You are a darling brave soldier!" said the fairy, drying her eyes. "Whatever are we to do? That horrid goblin will keep me prisoner for years if I don't tell him all the magic I know. But I daren't do that because he will use it for wicked things. If only I could send word to the Fairy Queen, she would send her army to rescue me!"

The soldier tried the door. It would not budge an inch! He looked round in despair. "Is there no way of getting out of here?" he said. "Oh fairy, I wish I could rescue you! I do, do wish I could, but I don't see how I can."

He went to the walls and knocked on them to see if any place was hollow. But no, they were all made of solid earth. Suddenly the fairy held up her hand and said, "Hush! I can hear something!"

They listened. The soldier could distinctly hear someone talking. "Who is it?" he cried.

"Shh!" said the fairy, excitedly. "It's some rabbits. They must have a burrow near this room. Oh soldier, if only we could dig in the walls a little way, I believe we would come to the burrow and then we could escape!"

The soldier whipped out his sword at once and began to cut the earth away in one of the walls. The soil fell down into the room, and soon he had made quite a passage. It was very tiring standing so long on one leg, but he didn't stop for a minute in case the goblin came back.

At last he had made such a big tunnel that he had to get into it to make it bigger at the other end. Suddenly his sword went right through the end of the tunnel into a rabbit's burrow! The soldier stumbled through and saw three frightened rabbits staring at him.

"Excuse me," said the soldier, "but the goblin has got a fairy prisoner in his room below. Will you help me to rescue her?"

"Yes!" said the rabbits, and they went down the tunnel with the soldier. But alas! When he peeped into the goblin's room he saw the ugly goblin there, raging round because the soldier had gone – and even as he peeped, the goblin picked up the weeping fairy and rushed out of the room with her. The rabbits and the soldier heard the door being bolted again.

"Oh!" said the soldier in dismay. "This is worse than ever! I have escaped but the fairy is still a prisoner. If only I could tell the Fairy Queen – but I don't know where she lives."

"We know!" cried the rabbits. "Come with us and we'll take you!"

In a trice the soldier hopped on to the

biggest rabbit's back and off they all went up the burrow, into the woods above, and over fields and hills. At last they came to a shining palace, gleaming in the moonlight. The rabbits ran up the steps,

and it was not long before the King and Queen had been awakened and knew all the story.

"Those wicked goblins!" cried the King, in a fury. "They need to be taught a lesson! My army shall march on them at once! Soldier, will you command them and be their captain? I have never known anyone as brave as you!"

"Oh, Your Majesty, it is very good of you to say so!" said the toy soldier, going red with pleasure. "But, you see, I have only one leg and cannot march. Also my uniform is in a dreadful mess. I should be ashamed to command your army."

"Pooh, that's easily put right!" said the King. "Where's my head carpenter? Tell him to make a brand-new leg at once. And where's my head painter? Tell him to come and paint the soldier a new uniform. I'll soon have you all right again, my brave captain!"

Well, just imagine that! The carpenter came along and made a fine new leg at once and fitted it on. Then he glued it very firmly, and the soldier found that he could walk, run and march just as well

as ever! Oh, wasn't he delighted! Then the painter gave him a most beautiful red coat and brilliant blue trousers, and touched up his black busby.

When the King was ready and all the army was drawn up outside the palace, the toy soldier strode out, a captain brave, fine and splendid. He took his place at the head and off they all marched.

It wasn't long before they came to the goblins' caves, and attacked the astonished and frightened goblins.

"Mercy! Mercy!" cried the goblins and fell on their knees, terrified. "We will give up the fairy. We did not mean any harm."

"Lock them up in their own caves," commanded the King. "Keep them prisoners there for a year. That will be a good punishment for them and keep them out of mischief!"

So all the goblins were locked up and the victorious army marched back again, with the little fairy riding in a golden coach beside the brave toy soldier.

And now he is head-captain of all the King's armies, and you should just see him marching about, his uniform shining and his sword gleaming brightly. His new leg is much better than his old one, and he is as happy as the day is long.

One day he is going back to Gerry's house to visit his old friends, the toys, to tell them all his adventures. But I don't believe they will know him. Do you?

Poor Mr Pop-Off

Mr Pop-Off walked happily down the street. He had done a good day's work and he was pleased with himself.

"Hi-ti-tiddley-ti!" he hummed. "I'm a very happy man. I've never had a day's illness in my life, I've as good eyes, ears and nose as ever I had, a dear little wife, and a cosy home. Hi-ti-tiddley-ti, I'm a very happy man."

Now just at that moment someone came up the street. Mr Pop-Off stopped his little song and stared hard.

"It's a little boy," he said. "But, oh dear, dear me – he looks like two to me! My eyes must be going wrong. Yes, he looks exactly like two boys. Two bodies, two heads, four eyes, four arms, four feet – oh dear, dear me! I'm seeing double, that's plain. I must get my eyes examined at once."

Well, he hadn't gone much further when he saw a little girl.

"Two again!" said Mr Pop-Off, going pale. "Two bodies, two heads, four eyes, four arms, four feet! Oh dear, dear me, this is a dreadful thing."

Then he saw a baby in a push-chair, and he mopped his forehead in despair.

"Two again!" he said. "This is dreadful, really dreadful. Yes, two heads with fluffy hair, two bodies, four feet, four hands. Oh dear, dear me!"

He walked home very quickly, not daring to look at anyone else in case they were two people also. When his wife came to the door he wouldn't look at her either, and she was so astonished.

"Why don't you smile at me and kiss me?" she asked.

"I'm afraid I'll see two of you if I do," said poor Mr Pop-Off. "My eyes are bad, my dear. I shall have to wear spectacles."

"Let me see them," said his wife. So Mr Pop-Off raised his head and looked at her to show her his eyes. And, good gracious me! He didn't see double this time, for there was only one wife looking at him.

How glad he was!

"Why, they're better again," he said in delight. "Perhaps it was just the cold weather that made them go wrong out-of-doors."

He forgot all about his eyes until the next day when he was coming home once more. Suddenly he began to see two children again. Yes, there were two boys eating apples.

"Two boys, two apples, two everything exactly the same," said poor Mr Pop-Off. "Why can't my eyes see just the one boy without making him into two? Oh dear, dear me, this is dreadful."

Then he caught sight of a girl coming down the street sucking a long stick of peppermint.

"Two girls, two peppermint sticks, two everything exactly the same," said Mr Pop-Off in despair.

Then he saw the baby sucking its dummy.

"Two babies, two dummies, two everything exactly the same!" said Mr Pop-Off, groaning, "I shall go straight to the eye-doctor and get a pair of glasses."

He went to Mr See-Well, the eye-man, and no sooner had he stepped into the shop than his eyes became all right again. He saw one of everything, and not two.

He explained his trouble to Mr See-Well, who promised to make him a fine pair of glasses and send them along the next day. Sure enough, he kept his promise, and the spectacles arrived just as Mr Pop-Off was about to go home.

Mr Pop-Off put them on. Then he set out to walk home. But would you believe it! He saw two boys again, exactly alike, two girls, and two babies!

"My eyes are wrong still," said Mr Pop-Off in despair. "These glasses are no good. I still see one boy as two, and one girl as two, and one baby as two. It is dreadful."

His wife was very upset when she heard all he had to say. "I'm afraid you will have an accident if your eyes go wrong like this when you are walking home," she said. "I shall come and fetch you tomorrow, and walk with you, dear."

So the next day she came to fetch him, just at six o'clock. They set out together, and Mr Pop-Off looked about him nervously, afraid every moment he would see double again.

Suddenly he saw the boy coming towards him.

"There!" he said, with a groan. "Do you see that boy? Well, he looks like two boys to me. And see – here comes a little girl. Well, she looks like two to me, both exactly alike, same hair, same dress, same everything. And look at this baby in the push-chair. It seems to me as if there were two there, both exactly alike. Oh dear, dear me, my eyes must be very bad indeed. To think my spectacles should be of no use, too!"

Then, to Mr Pop-Off's great surprise and annoyance, his little wife began to laugh.

How she laughed! She rolled about and held her sides, while tears trickled down her fat little nose and dripped on to the pavement. She said "Ha, ha, ha!" and "He, he, he!" and "Ho, ho, ho!" and then she began all over again. Mr Pop-Off really thought she had gone mad.

"What's the matter?" he asked in alarm. "What do you find to laugh at?"

"Oh dear, oh dear, oh dear!" laughed Mrs Pop-Off, drying her eyes. "You really are the funniest man I ever saw! Your eyes bad, indeed! Why, there's nothing

wrong with them at all!"

"Nothing wrong!" cried Mr Pop-Off. "Do you call seeing double nothing wrong, then? Well, I never did!"

"Mr Pop-Off!" said his wife, tapping him on the arm. "Tell me, have you never heard of twins in your life?"

"Twins? Yes, of course," said Mr Pop-Off. "But what have they got to do with my eyes going wrong?"

"Well, the children you've seen every

day are Mrs Twiddle's children," said Mrs Pop-Off. "She has three sets of twins, two boys, two girls and two babies, and they all go to call on their grandma at six o'clock. They are always dressed alike, and you can't tell one from another, for they are like peas in a pod. So you might have bought a hundred pairs of spectacles,

Mr Pop-Off, and they wouldn't have done your eyes any good! Oh my, oh my, you'll be the death of me, you will! Ho, ho, ho!"

She began laughing again, and after a minute Mr Pop-Off began too. The six children stared at them in surprise, and were delighted when Mr Pop-Off gave them each a pound.

"That's for being twins," said Mr Pop-Off. Then off he went home with his little wife, as happy as a sandboy once again.

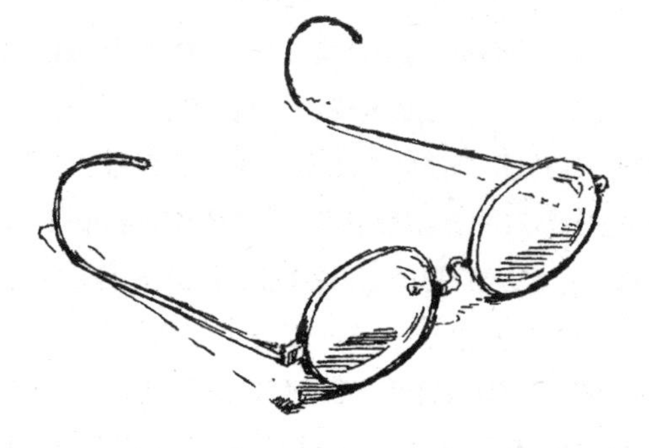

The Sparrow, the Frog, and the Duck

Once a green frog swam in a pond. He looked out for a moment and saw a little brown sparrow sitting in the sun on the bank.

The sparrow did not know that a great black cat was creeping up behind him, ready to pounce on him and catch him. No – there he sat, basking in the autumn sunshine, enjoying himself.

The frog saw the cat, and knew what was going to happen. He croaked to the sparrow, but the little brown bird only chirrupped back, and did not fly off.

The frog climbed up the bank to tell the sparrow – but he saw that he had no time. The cat was about to jump.

The frog jumped first! High in the air he went, just in front of the cat, who was most alarmed. She drew back, hissing, –

and the sparrow just had time to fly off quickly. The cat flung out her paw, but the bird was gone – and so was the frog! He jumped back into the water, *splash*!

The sparrow flew to a branch of a tree that leaned over the water and called to the frog.

"Frog! You saved my life! Thank you very much."

"Don't mention it, Sparrow!" said the frog, popping his blunt nose out of the water. "It was a pleasure to do such a thing."

The sparrow flew off, thinking of his good frog-friend. The frog dived down to the bottom of the pond and looked for water-grubs.

The next day the frog had a great shock. Some ducks came to the pond! Yes, great, fat, white ducks. The farmer's wife took them there, and they splashed into the water with glee.

"Plenty of food here!" cried the biggest duck. "Frogs, grubs, all kinds of water insects! Good!"

The frog was frightened. He didn't want to be eaten. He thought he had better escape while there was still time. So he swam to the other side. But a big duck was there, and if the frog had not dived quickly he would certainly have been caught.

The sparrow came to see his friend, but the frog did not dare to pop his nose

above the water to say how-do-you-do. The sparrow looked in surprise at the ducks.

"Quark, quark, quark!" said the biggest duck in a very deep voice.

"Quack, quack!" answered the others.

"Quark, quark, quark!" said the first duck, and tipped herself upside down to see what she could find on the bottom of the pond.

"What funny voices they have!" chirrupped the brown sparrow to himself. "How loud! How ugly! I wonder where my little frog-friend is. I do hope he is safe."

At that very moment the biggest duck swung herself the right way up again – and in her beak was the poor little green frog! His back legs stuck out of the duck's mouth, and he wriggled helplessly. The sparrow looked on in horror.

"Wait, wait!" he cried. "Don't swallow that frog you have in your beak! You don't want to spoil that marvellous voice of yours, do you, Duck?"

The duck stared at the sparrow. Marvellous voice! Ah, that sounded fine!

"I would so much like to hear you quack," said the sparrow, hopping to the end of the twig so that he was quite near to the duck. "You have a magnificent voice. Please let me hear it before you swallow that frog. It will, I am afraid, be spoilt when you have swallowed him, so pray quack first."

The duck swelled with pride. All the other ducks swam round the pond in astonishment. What was all this talk about fine voices?

"Quack, quack, quack, quack, quack!" they all cried together. "Quack, quack, quack, quack!"

"Yes – your voices are quite good," said the brown sparrow, nervously watching the frog's legs kicking in the duck's wide beak. "But this is the duck I want to hear. Ah – she has a voice that the King himself might envy!"

The duck swelled her throat for an extra fine quack. "Quark!" she said. "Quark! Quark, quark, quark!"

And as she quacked with all her might the frog shot right out of her mouth into the pond, *splash*! The other ducks

pecked at him quickly – but he was out of sight and at the bottom of the pond in a twinkling!

"Madam, your voice is simply wonderful!" cried the sparrow. "Do you mind if I fetch the King himself to hear it?"

"Quark, quark," answered the duck, delighted, and looked around for the frog. But he was gone. Yes – he was carefully and quietly clambering out of that pond under a bush on the far side! He hopped away to the hedge, and there he stayed until the brown sparrow came to tell him that the ducks had quite given up looking for him.

"Thank you for your help," said the frog gratefully. "I shall live here now, and find a damp place to sleep in for the winter. That pond is dangerous now the ducks have come."

"Live under that stone there," said the sparrow, pointing with his beak to a mossy stone nearby. "I will roost near you at night and frighten away any enemies. Then, when you wake in the spring, we can have some fine times together!"

And what about the vain duck? Well, she is still waiting for the King to come and hear her grand voice. You can hear her practising her song all day long, if you listen by the pond. "Quark, quark, quark!" she goes. "Quark, quark, quark!"

Sixpence for a Puppy

Once upon a time there was a boy called John. John was so pleased because Uncle Ben had been to see Mummy and Daddy, and when he said goodbye he gave John a silver sixpence. John had never had so much money before. He had a penny every Saturday, and sometimes Mummy gave him another penny if he went to post the letters for her.

But sixpence! A silver sixpence! That was a lot of money. John sat down in his chair and wondered what to spend it on. He didn't want to put it into his money-box – and besides, Uncle Ben had said he was to spend it on something he badly wanted. John thought of all the things he badly wanted. He wanted a new truck for his train. He wanted a new ball, because his old one had a hole in it. He wanted a book about aeroplanes.

But most of all he wanted a puppy! "I want a puppy so badly that I can't wait another minute now I have a whole sixpence of my own!" said John. "I shall go out and buy a new puppy. It shall be a dear little one, with a wag in its tail and a little pink tongue to lick me."

So he put his sixpence into his pocket, put on his coat, and went down to the village to spend his sixpence. He wondered where he could buy his puppy.

"I know the shop that sells dog-biscuits," said John to himself. "If they

sell dog-biscuits I expect they sell dogs too. I will buy my puppy there."

So into the shop he went. The man behind the counter smiled at him.

"What do you want this morning, young man?" he asked.

"I want a sixpenny puppy," said John.

"I'm very sorry," said the man, "but we don't sell puppies."

John went out of the shop feeling most disappointed. He wondered where to go next.

"I remember seeing a kitten sitting in the window of the newspaper man's shop once," he said to himself. "If they have kittens, they may have puppies."

So he went to the newspaper man's shop. The newspaper man was there, reading a book. He smiled at John when he came in.

"And what can I do for you this morning?" he said. "Have you come for your father's paper?"

"No," said John, "I've come to buy a sixpenny puppy."

"I'm so sorry," said the newspaper man, "but I don't sell puppies. I have a nice

sixpenny book all about dogs, though, if you'd like that instead."

"No, thank you," said John, and he went out feeling very disappointed again.

"Where shall I go to now?" he wondered. "Oh, I know! The toyshop! Why didn't I think of that before? How silly of me! They sell lots of toy animals, and I'm sure they must sell real ones too."

So he ran to the toyshop and went in. The shop girl smiled at him.

"What would you like today, John?" she said, for she knew him well. He always spent his Saturday penny in her shop.

"I want a sixpenny puppy, please," said John.

"I have a pretty toy puppy here," said the girl, and she put one on the counter.

"He squeaks if you press him in the middle."

"Oh, but I meant a real live puppy, not a toy one," said John.

"I'm very sorry, but I haven't any real ones," said the shop-girl. "We only sell toys."

John went out of the toyshop. He was so upset that he began to cry. This was very babyish of him, but he couldn't seem to help it. It was horrid to think that there might be a puppy somewhere waiting to be bought, and John had got a sixpence to buy him, and neither of them could find one another. A lady saw him crying, and she went over to him.

"What's the matter?" she said.

"I've got a sixpence to buy a puppy and I can't get one anywhere," said John, wiping his eyes.

"Dear me!" said the lady. "Now isn't this strange! I have five tiny puppies at home, and I want to find a nice little boy to give one to! And I've met you! Shall we go and ask your mother if she would like me to give you one of my little puppies? You see, I want someone kind who will

feed and brush and love the puppy – and I really think you are the right person!"

When John's mother heard about John trying to buy a puppy for sixpence in the shops, she laughed and kissed him. "You shall have one of Mrs Brown's puppies as she is so kind as to say she will give you one," she said. "Go along with a basket and get it now."

So John found a basket and went with Mrs Brown. He chose a little brown-and-white puppy with a very waggy tail and a long pink tongue that licked John's hand and made it very wet! John was so excited!

"Thank you very much, Mrs Brown,"

he said. “Here is my sixpence to pay for the puppy.”

“Oh, I am giving you the puppy, not selling it to you,” said Mrs Brown. “You see, I want a good home and a kind master for it. Keep the sixpence and buy a collar for the puppy and a rubber bone for him to chew. He will like that.”

So on the way home John went into the toyshop once again.

“I’ve got my puppy,” he told the girl there. “He is in this basket. Now I want to buy a red collar for threepence and a rubber bone for threepence too.”

The shop-girl gave him a beautiful red puppy collar and a fine rubber bone. She took John's sixpence, and the little boy ran home with the puppy, the collar and the bone.

"I'm so happy!" he shouted, as he ran indoors. "I've got my puppy, and I've spent my sixpence. Mummy, what shall I call my new dog?"

They called him Tubby, because he was so fat. You should just see him racing along with John! They do have some good times together, I can tell you!

Gee-Up, Old Clothes-Horse!

Once upon a time the two pixies, Diddle and Pompetty, went to buy themselves new suits to go to Dame Twiddle's party. They went to Mr Snip the tailor, and he fitted them out with a marvellous suit each.

Diddle had a red suit with green buttons, and Pompetty had a green suit with red buttons. They each had a black hat with a feather in it, so you can guess they looked very smart!

When they walked out of the shop they looked at one another and laughed.

"You look like the King of Diddle," said Pompetty.

"And you look as if you ought to be Lord High and Mighty Pompetty," said Diddle. "Let's pretend we are."

So they took a walk through the woods,

and sang as they went. This is what Diddle sang:

> "I'm the King of Diddle,
> Hie-tiddle-iddle-iddle!
> I've a palace tall and fair
> And a golden crown to wear,
> Oh, I'm the King of Diddle,
> Hie-diddle-iddle-iddle!"

Then Pompetty sang a little song he had made up. It went like this:

"Here comes Lord Pompetty,
  rich as can be,
Hey-derry, ho-derry,
  smick-a-smack-smee!
Look at me well,
  I'm as grand as ten kings,
I've castles and cabbages,
  riches and rings,
Oh, here comes Lord Pompetty,
  rich as can be,
Hey-derry, ho-derry,
  smick-a-smack-smee!"

"That's a good song of yours," said Diddle, "especially the bit about smick-a-smack-smee. But cabbages don't seem to go with castles somehow."

"No, they don't," said Pompetty. "But it was the only word I could think of just then."

They went on through the wood, singing their songs, and every one they met stopped and stared. Little elves bowed to them. Brownies cheered them. Diddle and Pompetty really did feel

very grand indeed.

But suddenly they met the old enchanter, Little-Eyes. He was always on the look-out for riches, and when he heard the song of the two pixies his little eyes gleamed.

"Stars and moon, if only I could catch these two rich fellows, and hold them prisoner, I could get a lot of money out of them," thought the enchanter to himself.

So he went up to them and bowed. "Sirs," he said, "I have a fine carriage here for sale. Such great men as yourselves might like to buy it."

"Well, no, thank you, we don't want a carriage today," said Diddle.

"We've plenty at home," said Pompetty, grandly and most untruthfully – but he was still pretending to be Lord Pompetty.

"Well, great sirs, will you not let me take you for a short ride?" said the artful enchanter. "Perhaps you may have a friend who would like to buy it."

Diddle and Pompetty had never ridden in a grand carriage in their lives. They simply longed to go in the enchanter's carriage. They could see it not far off between the trees – and it had four white owls for horses! Lovely!

"Well," said Diddle, "I don't mind if I do take a ride."

So the two pixies got into the blue carriage, the enchanter whipped up the owls, and off they went in the air, over the tops of the trees. It was very pleasant.

"I think we'd better go back now," said Diddle, after a while. "We're going to a party this afternoon and it wouldn't do to be late."

Little-Eyes the enchanter said nothing. He just whipped up his owls a bit faster. The two pixies suddenly felt scared. What was this old fellow up to? Surely he wasn't

Gee-Up, Old Clothes-Horse!

taking them away to keep? What good would that do him? Ah – but he thought they were a king and a lord! Of course! He meant to get money out of them.

Just then the owl-carriage dropped down to a big cottage standing on a hill by itself. The door opened; the owls flew in and took the carriage with them. It just got inside the door nicely. The door slammed shut behind it and the enchanter gave a laugh.

"Welcome!" he said to the pixies. "I've caught you nicely, Your Majesty Diddle, and Your Highness Pompetty. Now you won't be able to get away unless you promise to give me a castle to live in, and ten sacks of gold to spend."

The pixies stared at him in horror. "Don't be silly," said Diddle at last. "We're only ordinary pixies. We're not really grand people. We were only pretending. After we've paid for these suits, which were new today, we shan't have a penny."

"I don't believe that," said Little-Eyes. "I saw all the elves bowing to you, and heard the brownies cheering you in the wood. No – you won't trick me by pretending you are just ordinary pixies. I know you are rich and grand men."

Well, nothing that Diddle or Pompetty could say would make Little-Eyes believe they were ordinary pixies. It was so tiresome, because the pixies knew that they would not be able to go to the party if Little-Eyes wouldn't let them go.

"I'll leave you to think things over by yourselves," said the enchanter at last. "You can go into the kitchen. It's nice and warm there – and you needn't try to get out of the window because there's a spell on it so that it can't be opened. I shall lock the door."

So the two pixies found themselves prisoners in a warm kitchen. There certainly was a spell on the window, for it wouldn't move at all. Diddle and Pompetty stared at one another in dismay.

"We've been rather foolish," said Diddle in a small voice. "We shouldn't have been so vain. It looks as if we shall miss the party, Pompetty – so our new suits will be wasted."

"Even if we could get out of the window, we've got no way of getting home," said Pompetty gloomily. "We've no horse – no bird – no aeroplane."

They stared at the fire. A clothes-horse stood in front with some handkerchiefs and collars on it, drying. An idea came to Diddle and he gave a squeal.

"Pompetty! Do you know enough magic to make this clothes-horse come alive for a little while?"

"Yes!" shouted Pompetty, who was quite good at spells. He took a box from his pocket and dipped his finger into some ointment it held. He rubbed it carefully over the clothes-horse. Then the two pixies danced solemnly round it and sang a song of strange magic words – and as they sang and danced, peculiar things happened to the clothes-horse.

It grew a horse's head! It grew a long tail! Its legs grew longer and it began to paw the ground! It was a real clothes-horse now, that could whinny and shake

its mane and tail! The pixies jumped on its back and shouted in joy.

Just at that moment the enchanter opened the door to see what the noise was about – and that was the pixies' chance.

"Gee-up, old clothes-horse!" yelled Diddle, and the clothes-horse geed-up. It galloped at top speed to the door, knocked over Little-Eyes, and tore out of the cottage on its wooden legs. My, what a sight that was! The clothes-horse still wore the collars and handkerchiefs that had been drying on it, and it did look funny. The enchanter was quite frightened to see such a strange creature, and forgot all the magic spells he knew till the pixies were halfway home.

They galloped right to Dame Twiddle's on the clothes-horse, for it was time for the party. How every one stared to see them coming on such a strange steed!

"Whoa, horse! Whoa there!" shouted Pompetty to the clothes-horse, and the two pixies jumped off. Diddle was just about to tie it to the gatepost with some rope he had found when it tossed its funny head, whinnied loudly and galloped off to the west.

Nobody knows where it went to. Diddle thinks it will go to the moon and back again, and he hopes he will catch it once more when it comes back. But if I see it I shall catch it! Wouldn't you?

The Astonishing Curtains

Mary had a lovely doll's-house. Grandpa had made it for her birthday and it was quite empty. Grandma gave her five pounds to buy furniture for it, and Auntie Susan gave her one pound to buy curtains.

Mary went to the toyshop and spent the five pounds. She bought a little wooden table for the kitchen and two chairs to match. She bought a kitchen stove and dresser, and some tiny saucepans and a kettle.

She bought little beds for the bedrooms, and wardrobes and chairs. She even bought a dressing-table for the biggest bedroom of all. The dining-room had a round table, four chairs and a sideboard, and the sitting-room had a fine carpet, a sofa, three pretty chairs and a tiny table.

Well, you wouldn't think Mary could get

all those for five pounds, would you? But she did, because the toyshop was closing down and everything was half price, so she was able to buy twice as much.

"Don't buy the stuff for the curtains today," said her mother. "You'll have plenty to do arranging all the things you've bought. We will buy the curtain material another time, and then I will

help you to make them, and hang them up. You can keep Auntie Susan's pound until you want to buy the curtains."

Mary arranged all her new furniture in the doll's-house, and it did look nice. It took her two days to get it all in and to lay the carpets and rugs. Then she took out her one-pound piece, and decided to buy the stuff for the curtains.

She spun it on the floor – but, oh dear me, when it stopped spinning it rolled away and disappeared down a hole in the floor by the wall. Mary called her mother, but they couldn't get it.

"No, it's gone," said Mother. "It's a mouse-hole, I expect, and unless we have some boards taken up, you won't get your pound back again. I'm sure Daddy won't have the boards up just for that, so you must make up your mind that it's gone for good."

Tears came to Mary's eyes.

"What about the curtains for the doll's-house?" she said. "I've finished it all except for those – and Grandma and Auntie Susan are coming next week to see my house all finished."

"Well, you shouldn't have been so careless as to lose your pound," said her mother. "I told you to put it safely in your money-box."

She went out of the room and Mary sat down on the floor and cried. It really was too disappointing for anything. She did so badly want pretty red curtains to hang at the windows of the doll's-house.

That night, when the house was quiet, and Mary had gone to bed, the toys in the cupboard came trooping out. And dear me, they were so cross with the little clockwork mouse!

"It's all your fault that Mary lost her pound," the monkey said angrily.

"What do you mean?" asked the clockwork mouse in surprise.

"Well, your friend, the little brown mouse from the garden, made that hole to come indoors and visit you," said the monkey, pointing to the hole. "And it was down his hole that Mary's money went. If you hadn't wanted that mouse to come and see you, he wouldn't have made that hole, and Mary wouldn't have lost her pound!"

The clockwork mouse was dreadfully upset. He began to cry, and the toys tried to stop him, because they were afraid his tears might rust his spring.

"I w-w-wish I c-c-could get M-M-Mary some nice n-n-new c-c-curtains!" he sobbed. "I'm so s-s-sorry about it."

"If only we could get some stuff, I could make them on that little toy sewing machine Mary had for Christmas," said the biggest doll. "It wouldn't take me long, because I know quite well how to use it."

"Well, where can we get some stuff?" asked the clockwork mouse, eagerly. "I know Mary wanted red curtains – where can we get something that is red?"

"I know!" cried the teddy bear. "What about the red creeper leaves that grow over the garden shed? If we got some of those, we could make lovely curtains of them for Mary."

"But how can we get them?" asked the clockwork mouse.

"We'll ask your friend, the little brown garden mouse, to get them for us," said the doll. So when the mouse popped up through the hole, they told him all about Mary and the lost pound, and asked him to get the red leaves. First of all he tried to get the pound out of the hole, but he couldn't. When he found it was no use, he ran off to get the red creeper leaves. He came back with two beautiful ones in his mouth and then ran off for more.

The sewing machine began to hum as the doll made the curtains. As soon as a pair were made the teddy bear and the monkey took them to a window and put them up. You can't think how lovely they looked!

Just as the cock crowed at dawn, the last pair were finished and the toys went happily back to the toy cupboard.

And in the morning, when Mary came running downstairs, oh, what a surprise she had! She stood and stared at the doll's-house with its beautiful red curtains as if she really couldn't believe her eyes! And when she saw that they were made of red creeper leaves, she looked round at her smiling toys in wonder.

"You must have made them for me!" she said. "You darlings!" She hugged them all tightly, and they were as pleased as could be.

"Now the house is all ready for Grandma to see!" Mary cried. "And the curtains are the prettiest part of all!"

The Dog That Helped a Fairy

Bobs was a jolly little fox-terrier dog. He lived with Benny, his small master, and they had fine games together. Benny taught Bobs to sit up and beg, and to balance a biscuit on his nose. When Benny said "Paid for!" Bobs would toss his nose up, throw the biscuit into the air and catch it, very cleverly, in his mouth.

The two often went for long walks together. They were very fond of one another, and when Benny was naughty, and had been told off, Bobs would sit close to him and put his nose into Benny's hands. That was very comforting to Benny.

"I do wish you could talk, Bobs!" Benny would often say. "If only you could, how fine it would be! We should be able to be even greater friends then, because you could tell me all your thoughts and secrets, just as I tell you mine!"

But Bobs couldn't talk. He could whine, yelp, growl, wuff and bark, but he couldn't say a word. He often wished he could, for there were many things he would have loved to tell Benny.

One day Benny and Bobs went for a walk in Sandy Woods. Bobs loved that walk because there were so many rabbits about. It was most exciting to poke his nose down all the holes and smell rabbit, rabbit, rabbit!

Benny was looking for birds' nests. He never took any eggs, but he loved to see the sky-blue of the hedge-sparrows' eggs, or the pretty brown-red eggs of the robins. Bobs ran on in front. He knew of a fine rabbit-hole not far off, and he meant to have a good sniff down it!

On he ran, leaving Benny behind him – and suddenly he heard a most peculiar noise! It sounded like a parrot-screech, and after that came a sound of weeping. Bobs pricked up his silky black ears; then he ran quickly towards the strange sounds.

And, dear me, he saw a strange sight! A green-eyed witch was dragging a small fairy along by the wings! Bobs could hardly believe his eyes. Benny had often told him about fairies and witches and giants, but he had never in his little doggy life seen any before. And now here were two!

The witch was making the parrot-like screeching noises. She was quite delighted because she had caught a fairy.

The frightened little prisoner was weeping loudly. "Let me go! Let me go! You'll break my wings!"

"You shall come and be my servant and sweep and scrub my house for me!" screeched the green-eyed witch. "I have wanted a servant like you for a long time."

Then the small fairy caught sight of the surprised dog peeping between the trees, and she called to him. "Help! Help! Little dog, come and save me!"

The witch looked round and saw Bobs. She glared at him and cried "If you come near me I'll turn you into a bone!"

Bobs was frightened. He didn't at all want to be turned into a bone. Why, he might be eaten by another dog, then! But the poor little fairy's crying nearly broke his kind little heart. He really must help her!

So he rushed up to the angry witch and – would you believe it – he bit her on the leg! She gave a loud squawk, dropped the little fairy and hopped round and round, holding her leg, and shouting, "I'll turn you into a bone, yes, I will, I'll turn you into a bone!"

"Quickly!" whispered the fairy into Bobs's ear. "Run away with me before she remembers the spell to turn you into a bone!"

"Jump on my back!" wuffed Bobs, and the fairy understood his barks quite well. She slipped softly on to his hairy back, and off he galloped at top speed. The old witch saw him and cried out a string of strange, very magic words. It was the spell to change Bobs into a bone!

But he was out of sight before the spell could work properly, and how glad he was! Still, something strange seemed to have happened to his tail. He couldn't move it. Whatever was the matter with it? It wouldn't wag properly.

"Oh dear, your poor tail has changed

into a bone!" said the fairy suddenly. "A bit of the spell must have acted after all. What a good thing we got away when we did!"

"Wuff, wuff!" said Bobs, sadly, looking at his strange bone-tail. Whatever would Benny say when he saw it? What would other dogs say? Bobs felt very unhappy.

The fairy saw his ears drooping sadly, and she slipped off his back and hugged him. "Don't look so miserable," she said. "Cheer up! Come along to Pixieland with me, and I'll get my aunt, Dame Tweedles, to put your tail right again!"

She took hold of Bobs's collar and led him to a very big rabbit-hole, the biggest that Bobs had ever seen. And just as he was about to go down it what should he hear but Benny's whistle! Then he heard Benny calling him.

"Bobs! Bobs! Where are you?"

"Quick! Come with me, or you'll never get your tail right!" said the fairy, pulling him down the hole. "I'll take you back to Benny afterwards."

So Bobs disappeared down the very large rabbit-hole with the fairy, wondering what Benny would think when he didn't go running to him as usual.

Now, Benny just happened to come down the path as Bobs was disappearing down the hole. He was most astonished to see Bobs running down a rabbit-hole instead of coming when he was called. He stood and stared, wondering if Bobs would come back – but he didn't.

"Well, how strange!" said Benny. He bent down and looked into the hole – and then he saw a most surprising thing! Not far down that dark hole was a lamp, shining brightly! Whoever heard of a lamp

hung in a rabbit-hole? Benny never had, and he guessed at once that it was not a real rabbit-hole. There must be something magic about it!

He bent down and looked into it. It was a very big hole. It was really big enough for him to get down it, with a squeeze. He wondered if he should.

Then, far down the hole, he heard a little bark.

"That's Bobs!" he said. "Why didn't he come when I whistled to him? I wonder whether some witch has got hold of him. Oh dear! I must go down and see. I should have to save him if he was in danger."

So down that big hole Benny squeezed himself. Soon he came to the lamp – and then he saw that the hole widened out into a passage set with shallow steps that went down and down.

"This is a real adventure!" thought the little boy, going down the steps. He went down about a hundred and then he came to a low, stout door set across the passage. A lamp shone over it, and on the door was printed one word in big letters: PUSH.

So Benny pushed and the door swung open. To the little boy's enormous surprise he was looking out on a sunshiny village, whose pretty little cottages had thatched roofs and windows set with small diamond-panes.

"Well, who would have thought that such a place could be down at the bottom of a big rabbit-hole!" thought Benny in surprise. He stepped through the door, and looked round. There were many small fairies, pixies and gnomes going about their business, some with shopping baskets, some with bags. They didn't seem at all surprised to see Benny.

"Please, have you seen a small fox-terrier dog?" asked Benny, stopping a pointy-eared pixie.

"Yes, it went down that way," said the little creature, pointing down the village street. Benny went on, looking everywhere for Bobs. But he couldn't see him.

So he asked a gnome, and the gnome said, yes, he had seen a dog going to Hollyhock Cottage, not far down the lane. So off went Benny again.

Very soon he came to Hollyhock Cottage. He knew it must be, because although there was no name on the gate, great red and pink hollyhocks grew all round the walls.

Benny stopped and listened – yes, he

could quite well hear little wuffs and barks from inside the cottage. Bobs must be there!

He whistled loudly and waited. No Bobs came. He whistled again. Still no Bobs, but once more he heard the wuffs and barks. Bobs must be inside, and someone must be keeping him prisoner, or surely he would come running out to Benny!

The little boy crept round to the back of the cottage. There was a window there and he peeped in. What a strange sight he saw!

Bobs was standing in the middle of a ring of white chalk. Benny stared at his dog's tail, for it was just like a long butcher's bone! Benny suddenly felt angry! Were they doing some horrid magic to his dear little dog? How had his nice tail got like that?

He saw a little fairy stroking Bobs's head, and on the other side of the chalk ring stood an old dame, a bright red shawl wrapped round her shoulders. She was chanting a song made of strange words. Benny knew they were magic.

"I must rescue Bobs!" he thought. "Surely they are weaving a spell over

him, and he will be turned into something horrid. Bobs, Bobs!"

Calling his dog loudly he flung open the window and jumped inside. The fairy screamed and the old woman stared in astonishment. Bobs stood quite still for he was under a spell and couldn't move.

"Don't go into the magic ring!" begged the fairy, hanging on to Benny's arm. "Please don't! If you do you'll spoil the magic, and we shan't be able to make your dog's tail right again."

"Oh," said Benny, stopping. "Are you

trying to help him, then? I thought you were working a horrid spell on him."

"Of course not!" said the old dame, indignantly. "We are trying to make his bone-tail disappear and his own tail grow again. Watch now, and keep quiet."

So Benny watched, and as he stood there and looked, he saw Bobs's curious bone-tail gradually fade away into a sort of mist. For a minute the little dog stood in the ring with no tail at all – and then, to Benny's delight, his own hairy tail began to grow, and at last it was all there – and all of a sudden it began to wag!

Bobs leaped out of the magic ring and jumped up at Benny in joy. "Wuff, wuff, wuff!" he barked.

"How did you get here, and what has happened, Bobs?" asked Benny, patting the excited little dog.

"Wuff, wuff, wuff!" barked Bobs.

"Oh, I do wish you could tell me how you got here and why!" said Benny.

"Can't you understand what he is saying?" asked the fairy in surprise. "I can understand his wuffs and barks quite plainly."

"Well, I can't!" said Benny. "I've often wished I could. That's the only thing that comes between Bobs and me – he can understand all I say, but I never know what he is barking."

"Bobs," said the fairy, turning to the little dog who at once licked her small hand. "Bobs, I want to give you a reward for helping me to get away from that horrid green-eyed witch. Listen now – would you like me to give you a proper voice, like Benny's?"

"Wuff, wuff!" barked Bobs, jumping round everyone in great delight.

"Bobs says he would like to be able to talk to you," said the fairy, beaming at Benny. "Would you really like him to?

You would be able to talk to each other as much as you liked, whenever you liked."

"Oh, yes, I'd like that more than anything else in the world!" said Benny at once, his heart beating in excitement.

"Very well," said the fairy. "Aunt Tweedles, would you give me a talking spell, please?"

The old dame went to a drawer and opened it. She took out a round box and

slid off the lid. Inside were a great many little blue pills. She took one out and gave it to Benny.

"Give this to your dog before he goes to sleep tonight," she said. "Then in the morning he will be able to talk as you do. But remember this – he must only talk to you. If he tries to talk to anyone else his voice will go and never come back!"

Benny took the pill and thanked the old dame and the fairy very much.

Then he and Bobs went to the strange tunnel and made their way back to the wood. They were both so excited that they could hardly go fast enough!

That night Benny gave Bobs the pill and the little dog swallowed it whole. He wuffed, but didn't say a word. His voice hadn't yet grown!

But the next morning when Benny went to see him, what a wonderful surprise!

"Good morning, Benny!" said a gruff doggy voice. "I can talk! I can talk! And first let me say something I've always wanted to say to you."

"What is that?" asked Benny, delighted.

"I love you, little master, and I think

you are the finest person in the world!" said Bobs, jumping up to lick Benny's ear.

Well, wasn't that a lovely thing to hear from his dog? Benny was so pleased that he didn't know what to say. But very soon the two were chattering nineteen to the dozen, which means that they both talked at once, without stopping, for a very long time!

I know Bobs quite well – but I've never asked him to talk to me. It would be such a pity if he lost his funny, doggy voice, wouldn't it! So if ever you meet him, don't try and make him talk, will you?

The Christmas Tree Party

The children across the road were going to have a party. Janey knew, because she had seen an enormous Christmas tree arriving there, and she had seen a most beautiful Christmas cake being taken in, too, with candles all round it!

Janey wished she knew the children across the road, but she didn't. Janey didn't go to their school, and their mother wouldn't let them play with children they didn't know. So Janey just had to watch them and wonder about them – but she did wish she knew them, and could play games with them and go to their lovely, lovely parties!

"Mummy!" she said. "Look! The children across the road are going to have a party. I can see somebody putting lights and ornaments on the Christmas tree in the front room."

"Horrid, stuck-up children!" said Janey's brother. "They think themselves too good for us! I hope they have a horrid party!"

"Don't be unkind, Robin," said Mother. "They look very nice children to me."

"I'm going to watch what happens," said Janey. "If only they don't draw their curtains I can see everything plainly. I believe they are going to have tea in the front room too – I can see someone putting a big white cloth over a long table."

Janey watched for a long time. It did seem as if the party was going to be a beautiful one! Janey counted how many chairs were round the table – sixteen! Plates of sandwiches and cakes and buns and bowls of jellies and trifles. And right in the very middle of the table was the big Christmas cake, but the candles would not be lit until teatime.

"A Christmas tree party is the very best kind of party," said Janey to herself. "Oh, I do believe the children's mother is going to put all the presents on the tree now!"

So she was! The tree reached almost to the ceiling, and already had dozens of lights on it, and some bright, shiny ornaments and coloured balls. Now the mother was hanging dolls and engines and books and motor-cars and all kinds of exciting toys on it. Janey felt so excited herself that she had to jump up and down on the chair she was kneeling on!

"Any one would think you were going to the party yourself!" said Robin grumpily. "Can't you keep still?"

"No, I can't," said Janey. "It's all so exciting. Do come and watch, Robin."

"No, thank you," said Robin. "If I can't go to a party I don't want to watch other people going to it!"

"They're arriving!" cried Janey. "Here's a car with two little girls in it. One has a blue party frock and the other has a yellow one, and they both have ribbons in their hair and blue capes. And here come two boys walking down the street with their father. And here's another car – with three children and their mother. Oh, how excited they must feel!"

Janey watched all the children run up the path and go into the house. She hoped they would go into the front room, but they didn't.

"They must be playing games before tea in the room at the back," she told Robin. "What fun it will be to watch them come and have tea!"

There was very little to see after that, for no one came into the front room at all. The tea was ready, and the Christmas tree was waiting with its lights twinkling. Everyone was playing musical chairs with the children in the back room.

Janey sat and looked at the house opposite, loving the firelight that shone over the tea-table, and trying to see all the presents that hung on the big Christmas tree.

And then she noticed a very peculiar thing. The Christmas tree seemed to be falling over a bit. Yes – it was certainly slanting forward. How strange!

Janey watched, half scared. The tree tilted over a little more – it seemed to be falling towards the tea-table. It would spoil all the cakes and the jellies – it would

crush that beautiful Christmas cake! It must be too heavy for its tub. It was slowly falling, falling over!

"Robin! Look!" cried Janey. "The Christmas tree is falling over! Everything will be spoilt!"

"And a good thing too," said unkind Robin, who hated to see anyone having things he hadn't got. "Let it fall and break everything up!"

"Oh no, no, no!" cried Janey. "Oh no! It is too beautiful to be spoilt, and the children will be so unhappy! I shall go and tell them!"

And before Robin could say a word more the little girl shot out of the room, out of the front door, and across the street! She banged at the door there and when the mother came to open it in surprise, Janey told her why she had come.

"Your Christmas tree is falling down!" she cried. "It's spoiling itself and the lovely tea-table! I saw it from my window. Oh, quick, come and stop it!"

She and the mother ran into the front

room and were just in time to save the big Christmas tree from toppling over altogether! Nothing had been spoilt – but Janey was only just in time! The father came running in, and very soon he had the tree upright again, safely packed in its tub, and weighted down with some big stones.

"Well!" said the mother, looking at Janey. "What a lucky thing it was for us that you were watching the tree! Thank you so much."

"I've been watching everything," said Janey. "It was so exciting – seeing all the table laid with those lovely things – and watching the children come – and seeing you hang the presents on the tree. It was almost as good as coming myself. I'm glad I saved the tree for you."

"Are you the little girl that lives over the road?" asked the mother. "My children have often said they would like to know you. Let's run across the road to your mother and see if she will let you come to the party! One little girl hasn't come because she has a cold, so we have an empty place. It would be so nice if you could come!"

Well, think of that! Janey could hardly believe her ears! She took the mother's hand and they ran across the road. In a few minutes Janey's mother had heard all about how Janey had saved the Christmas tree from falling on to the tea-table, and Janey was putting on her pink party frock and brushing her hair in the greatest excitement!

Robin stood and watched. How he wished he had been as kind as Janey! If only he had run across with her and saved the tree, perhaps he would have been asked too. But he had been jealous and sulky – and that never brings treats or surprises, as kindness does!

Janey went to the party, and oh, what a fine one it was! All the children were told how Janey had saved the party and they thought she was wonderful.

And what do you think Janey had off the Christmas tree? Guess! She had the beautiful fairy doll off the very top, because every one said she ought to have the nicest present of all. Wasn't she lucky? But she really did deserve that doll, didn't she?

Now she is great friends with the children across the road, and so is Robin. They play together every Saturday and go to tea once a week. It was a good thing that Janey watched the party that afternoon, wasn't it?

Claws for the Cat

The toy cat was sad. She had a fine long tail just like a real cat. She had good whiskers. She had nice pointed ears and green eyes.

But she hadn't any claws. The real cat had plenty. She had shown them to the toy cat.

"Look," she said, and stretched out her paw, showing her sharp, curved claws. "See those? They're my claws. I'm sorry for you because you haven't any. You're not a real cat. You're only a toy cat without claws."

The toy cat often turned up her soft paws and looked at the underneath of them. It was true, she had no claws there at all. She wondered if they would grow. But they didn't.

"They never will," said the teddy-bear,

"so don't expect them to. And don't be sad about it. It doesn't matter."

But somehow it did matter to the toy cat. She looked sad and miserable. She wouldn't play. She kept hoping and hoping that claws would grow, but, of course, they never did.

"What shall we do for the toy cat?" said the monkey, in alarm. "She's getting so thin and miserable. Anyone would think her sawdust was leaking, she's so thin. What shall we do about it?"

"It's her birthday soon," said the bear. "Let's give a party for her, that may cheer her up. And we'll give her a few presents.

She might like a red bow and a blue bow, and perhaps a new saucer to pretend to drink from."

So they planned a party – but the toy cat didn't really feel happy about it. She didn't want a party. She didn't want bows or a saucer. She wanted claws.

And then one day, the monkey saw some claws! He was out in the garden with Helen, his little mistress, and she had him sat down by the rose-bed. There were still a few roses out, and the monkey liked the smell of them.

So, when Helen had gone indoors to fetch something, he got up and leaned over a rose to smell it. And then he saw the claws!

"Good gracious me!" said the monkey, in the greatest surprise. "Claws! Claws growing on a stalk! Claws growing all the way up the rose stems! What an extraordinary thing!"

He looked at the big, curved prickles on the rosebushes and scratched his head. He was sure that they were claws. The rosebush had so many of them. Surely it could spare a few for the toy cat.

"Rosebush," said the monkey in an excited voice, "could you spare twenty of your claws for a toy cat who doesn't have any? Please say yes."

The wind blew in the rosebush and the monkey thought he heard a whispered "Yes-s-s-s-s!" He was pleased.

He broke off a prickle, and then another and another. Soon he had twenty sharp, curved claws in his pockets. He hoped Helen wouldn't find them.

She didn't. She carried him indoors without guessing that his pockets were full of rose thorns! He could hardly wait till she had gone out of the room before he told everyone the news.

"I've got some claws for the toy cat. I have really! Look!"

They all looked. The toy cat gave an excited mew. "How marvellous! They are claws! Quick, put them in my paws!"

So, one by one the new claws were pressed into the toy cat's four paws, five in each, just like the real cat had. The toys were most excited about it.

"I've got claws, I've got claws!" cried the toy cat in delight, and she held up her paw to show everyone the curved claws there. They looked so real.

The real cat came in after a bit and she had to see the claws too. She was just

about to say that they were only rose prickles when she stopped. She didn't want to hurt the toy cat's feelings. Let her think they were real, proper claws if she wanted to!

"I suppose that's where you got your claws from too," said the toy cat, happily. "Wasn't it a good thing the monkey saw them on the rose stems? I do feel pleased. Now I shall enjoy my birthday party and everything."

So she did, and you should just have seen her holding her teacup, with all her claws showing well. But I don't somehow think she will use them for scratching, do you?

Have you a toy cat? Well, maybe you can give her claws too, if you ask the rosebushes for a few!

Mother Dubbins and her Clever Duck

There was once a poor old woman who lived with Waddles, her duck, in a tiny cottage at the end of Hazel Village. She had very little money, hardly enough to live on. All her small savings were kept in a long red stocking and hidden behind the big clock on the mantelpiece.

One day Mother Dubbins came home from shopping and went to put a penny in the red stocking. But, dear, oh dear! It wasn't there! Someone had stolen it.

The old woman was in a terrible way. She hunted here and she hunted there. She turned everything in her cottage upside down but it was of no use – she couldn't find the stocking in which were all her savings.

To make things worse it was the day

on which she had to pay her rent! What should she do when the landlord came? Would he give her time to pay, or would he turn her out?

The landlord was a horrid man. He was very unkind to old Mother Dubbins when he heard her tale.

"I don't believe you!" he said. "You bring me the money today, or I'll turn you out of your cottage and let someone else have it!"

Then he stamped off. Mother Dubbins knew quite well that she couldn't pay

him any money, and at first she could not think of what to do, for she was too proud to go and ask her friends for help. Indeed, they were almost as poor as she was.

She sat down and thought for a little while. Then she stood up and began to pack a few things in a bundle. She had made up her mind what to do.

"I shall go and seek my fortune," she said. "Lots of people do that. It is true that it is mostly young folk who go seeking fortunes, but I can think of no reason why I should not do so too. I shall go to the unkind landlord and tell him that he can sell my furniture, which will pay his rent."

So the brave old woman tied on her tall hat, put her bundle over her shoulder and went down the path to the front gate. In the garden was her duck. It was a fine, big bird, very plump and white, for Mother Dubbins loved it and took great care of it.

"Oh dear!" she said. "Who will look after Waddles the duck? Poor old Waddles, you must say goodbye to your mistress, for she is going to seek her fortune."

Then the duck did a surprising thing. It quacked very loudly, and Mother

Dubbins suddenly found that she could understand duck-language, though she never had before.

"Take me with you, old woman," said the duck. "I am fond of you, and would like to go with you. I may even help you, for I am wiser than you think. Also I can carry you on my back for I am big and you are small."

"Bless us all!" cried Mother Dubbins. "Now who would have thought that a duck could talk so sensibly? Well, Waddles, I will take you with me, and if you think you can carry me I shall be glad, for I am not used to walking."

"Get on my back now," said the duck, and she waddled over to Mother Dubbins. The old woman seated herself comfortably on the bird's soft back, and found that it was exactly right for her. She tied her bundle round the duck's neck, and then the two set off.

First she went to the landlord, and told him what she was going to do.

"You are a mean old man not to let me have time to pay you," she said. "But you can have my furniture, and that will pay the rent. I and my duck are now going to seek our fortunes."

"Ho ho!" laughed the landlord. "That is a funny joke! Ho ho!"

The duck looked at the scornful landlord and then suddenly jerked out her head. The man found himself pushed right off his feet, for the duck's powerful beak gave him a mighty blow in the waist. He went *splash*! into a puddle, and sat there, very much astonished. Everybody round laughed heartily, for no one liked the landlord.

"Quack, quack, quack, right on his back!" said the duck.

"This is a good beginning," said the old woman. "I can see you are going to look after me well, Waddles."

They set off again, and all day long they travelled. Mother Dubbins didn't get at all tired, for the duck's back was very soft and comfortable. In fact she almost fell asleep, but she wouldn't let herself do that for she was afraid of falling off.

After two days they came to a small town. The old woman stayed at an inn, and told everyone how clever her duck was.

"She has told me she will help me to make my fortune," said Mother Dubbins.

"What do you think of that?"

"Can she cure deafness?" asked a man who was very deaf. "I should like to be able to hear, so perhaps your wonderful duck could cure me."

"Can you do that, Waddles?" asked Mother Dubbins, turning to the duck.

"Quack, quack, quack, quack, take a feather from my back," said the duck.

The old woman pulled a feather from her duck's back and touched the man's ears with it. At once he shouted in delight, and danced about gladly.

"I can hear, I can hear!" he cried. "I hear the birds singing, and the water-mill going round, I hear the children laughing, and the wind sighing! That is truly wonderful!"

But do you know, the ungrateful man wouldn't pay a penny piece to Mother Dubbins for giving him his hearing!

"No, no," he said. "You can't make me deaf again, and if you did, I wouldn't pay you!"

Then he ran off chuckling, and told his wife all that had happened.

"Quack, quack, quack, I'll get my own back!" said the duck.

"But how?" asked Mother Dubbins, dolefully. "We can't make him pay. We shall never make our fortunes at this rate, Waddles."

The duck went off by herself and visited the man's wife. The poor woman could not speak, and had never been able to since the time she was eight years old.

"Quack, quack, quack, quack, would you like your language back?" asked the duck.

The woman stared at the wonderful bird in surprise. Never had she heard a duck speak before, and at first she was too astonished to make any sign in reply.

Then she nodded her head.

Waddles pulled out a feather from her

wing, and gave it to the woman. As soon as she touched it she began speaking, for her tongue was able to move again.

"I can speak, I can speak!" she cried. "Oh, how wonderful, dear duck! I will tell my husband when he comes home, and he will reward you!"

Just at that moment the man himself arrived. He looked most surprised to hear his wife speaking, and he in his turn told her that he had got his hearing back.

"Give the duck a gold piece," said the woman. "She deserves it."

"Not I!" said the ungrateful man, and turned away laughing. The duck said nothing more, but went waddling back to her mistress.

Now since the woman had got her speech back, she felt that she must talk every minute of the day and night. Clack-clack-clack, went her tongue, and soon her husband became very tired of it.

"When I got my hearing back, it was not that I might listen to your tongue all day long!" he said angrily.

"Oh, you horrid, unkind man!" cried his wife, and she straightaway began to scold him hard. She followed him into the yard, and scolded him there. She ran after him down the street, and scolded him there, and she scolded him long after they were in bed and he wanted to sleep.

That was quite enough for the man. Next day he went to the inn where Mother Dubbins was staying, and begged her to get the duck to take away his wife's voice.

"Not I!" said Mother Dubbins. "You didn't pay me a penny for helping you, and you can't expect me to help you now."

"Quack, quack, quack, quack, would you like your deafness back?" asked the duck, suddenly.

"Oh, yes, anything to get away from my wife's tongue!" cried the man.

"You must pay two gold pieces then," said old Mother Dubbins.

The man sighed heavily, and took two gold pieces from his pocket.

"I have been foolish," he said. "If I had paid you one gold piece yesterday, I could have got my hearing back and never have heard my wife's voice, for you would not have given it to her. Now I must pay you two gold pieces to lose my hearing again! But as I shall certainly go mad if I hear my wife scolding me day and night, there is nothing else to be done!"

"Mean people always pay dearly in the end," said Mother Dubbins. She took another feather from the duck and touched the man's ears. In a trice he had got his deafness back, and went to his home, glad that he could no longer hear his wife's scolding voice.

"This is the beginning of our fortune,"

said Mother Dubbins as she care
put the two gold pieces away into
bag. "Now we shall be on our way again, Waddles."

They travelled on together until they came to a dark wood. Mother Dubbins was tired, so she slid off the duck's back and prepared to rest for the night.

Now near by there lived a great robber in a cave. He had much gold in bags, and was feared by all the country folk around. He was half a giant, and when he wished to rob anyone, he found it the easiest thing in the world.

He heard Mother Dubbins talking to her duck and came out to see who was near. When he saw the fine, fat duck he thought that here was a splendid supper for him!

"What are you doing here?" he roared at Mother Dubbins. "No one is allowed near my cave. You must go, old woman, and to punish you I shall take your duck and eat her for my supper!"

"Oh, please excuse me," said Mother Dubbins, getting up in a hurry. "I had no idea I was trespassing. Pray let us go on our way safely. As for the duck, she is no ordinary bird, and I could not let her be eaten!"

But the robber took no notice of her words. He simply picked up the duck and took her off to his cave. Mother Dubbins was frightened, but she followed bravely, determined to rescue her duck if she could.

"Quack, quack, quack, quack, do not fear, I'll soon be back!" called the duck as the robber took her off.

Soon the giant arrived at his cave, and he made up a roaring fire, meaning to

cook the duck at once.

"You're the fattest bird ever I saw!" said the robber, rubbing his hands over the duck's soft back. "You'll make a fine supper for me!"

But, dear me, when he tried to take his great hands off the duck's back, he couldn't! They were stuck there as fast as if they had been glued!

"Quack, quack, quack, put a feather down his back!" called the duck. At once Mother Dubbins ran in and took a feather from the duck. Then she stuck it down the robber's neck and waited to see what would happen next, for she knew that the feathers were full of magic.

Soon a curious thing happened to the giant-like robber. He suddenly began to grow small! In a short time he was no bigger than Mother Dubbins herself, and then he was even smaller.

"Stop, stop!" he cried. "What is happening to me? Are you a witch, old woman? Let me go back to my own size again!"

But he went on growing smaller and smaller, and then, when he was no bigger than a six-year-old child, Mother Dubbins pulled the feather out from his neck.

"You are too small to do any harm," she said. "You will never be able to rob people again! That is a good punishment for you!"

The old woman settled down in the comfortable cave and made the robber wait on her. He could not do anything but obey her, for all his giant-like strength was gone.

It was not long before the country folk missed the giant-robber and they came peeping around the cave to see where he was, for all of them hoped he had gone to some other place and would leave them alone.

They were amazed when they saw him! At first they could not believe their eyes when they saw the little dwarf-like man running about obeying Mother Dubbins.

"My clever duck did it," said Mother Dubbins. "Perhaps you had all better come and see whether any of the things here belong to you. There is plenty of furniture in the cave, and I have found many bags of gold."

Soon all the people who had been robbed came to the cave, and they were very glad when they found their own belongings there.

"We will give you twenty pieces of gold for your good help," said they, and Mother Dubbins was delighted. She put the gold away in her bundle.

"We certainly are making our fortune!" she said to the duck.

Off they went again, and found many adventures up and down the countryside. The duck earned scores of gold pieces, and the old woman's bag began to be quite heavy.

Then one day there came a message from the King.

"His Majesty wishes to see your clever duck," said the messenger.

Mother Dubbins, very proud, mounted Waddles again, and made her way to the city where the King lived.

She was taken to the throne room, and when the King saw her coming in with her great duck, he laughed.

"Welcome!" he said. "You are a strange couple, truly. I hear you are seeking your fortune, old woman."

"That is true," said Mother Dubbins,

curtsying. "With the help of my good friend the duck, I am saving up many gold pieces."

"I want your help," said the King. "Can your duck find things that are lost or stolen?"

"Yes," said Mother Dubbins, and the duck answered too.

"Quack, quack, quack, quack, what you've lost I'll soon get back!" she said.

"Wonderful, wonderful," said the King, staring in admiration at the duck. "Well, I'll tell you all about it. Have you heard of the golden wishing-wand that a powerful fairy once gave to my great-great-grandfather, Mother Dubbins?"

"Oh, yes," said the old woman. "But surely, that is not lost, is it?"

"I fear it is stolen," said the King, sorrowfully. "I was holding a party a week ago, and I had twenty guests. I took out the magic wand to show them, and let them each handle it. Well, before it had gone halfway round the table, it had vanished, and no one knew where it was! What I want to find out is – who took the wand?"

"Quack, quack, quack, quack, don't you fret, I'll get it back," said the duck.

Then she and the old woman went out to make their plans. Soon Mother Dubbins went to the King again.

"Give another party, and ask exactly the same guests," said Mother Dubbins. "Say that you are giving it in honour of my clever duck. Tell everyone that they may stroke and pat her, for she will bring them good luck. But also say that if a thief pats her, it always makes my duck quack very loudly indeed. Then we shall see what we shall see."

The King did not know at all how this would find the thief for him, but he consented to do what Mother Dubbins advised. He sent out the invitations, and the guests all came, eager to see the wonderful duck.

Waddles had a beautiful blue bow tied round her neck, and stood in the middle of the King's hall. Everyone crowded round and admired her.

"Stroke her if you like," said the King. "She will bring you good luck. Only thieves and robbers must beware of touching her, for their hands always make her call out loudly."

So the duck had plenty of patting and stroking, but although the King waited patiently to hear if the duck cried out, she make no sound at all.

"Quack, quack, quack, quack, take your hands from off my back!" suddenly said the duck to everyone. So they all stopped patting her, and stood back in astonishment.

"Show me your hands," said Mother Dubbins, coming up to the guests. Everybody turned their hands palm upwards in surprise – and dear me, what a very peculiar thing – they were all as white as chalk!

Mother Dubbins looked at everyone's chalky hands, and then she suddenly came to a pair that were pink, and had no chalk on at all.

"Here is the man who stole your magic wand, Your Majesty," she said to the puzzled King. At once two stalwart footmen took hold of the thief's collar, and held him tightly.

"What! Sir Oliver Sly!" cried the King. "Can it really be you who took my magic wand?" Then he turned to Mother

Dubbins. “How do you know?” he said.

“Look at his hands,” said the old woman. “His are the only pair not white with chalk. I filled my duck’s back feathers with powdered chalk, for I knew that the only man who would not stroke her would be the thief, because he would not dare to in case Waddles quacked loudly at him! All the others patted her gladly, and unknowingly chalked their hands.

Search Sir Sly's house, and you will find your wand!"

"What a clever duck!" cried the King. "Footmen, lock Sir Sly up in prison, and then send soldiers to search his house!"

The frightened courtier was hauled off, and his house was thoroughly searched. The magic wand was found locked away in a cupboard and was taken to the King, who was delighted to have it back again.

"Your fortune is made," he said to the old woman. "Here is a big bag of gold for you. Now return to your village, Mother Dubbins, and settle down there happily, for you have enough riches to last you for the rest of your life."

"Thank you, Your Majesty," said Mother Dubbins, gratefully. "I shall do as you say."

She and the duck took their way back to the village they had come from. Mother Dubbins was excited to think that she was going home again at last, and she wondered if anyone else had got her little cottage.

At last she arrived. Everyone came flocking out to greet her, for they had heard of her fame. Only the mean landlord did not come, for he was angry to think she had come back rich.

Mother Dubbins' cottage was empty, for no one would rent it from the unkind landlord after she had gone. As for her furniture, she did not bother about that, for she had plenty of money to buy more.

Soon her little cottage was furnished, and very pretty it looked. Then Mother Dubbins gave a grand party and invited everyone in the village to it. Even the horrid landlord got an invitation, but he didn't dare to accept it because he was afraid the duck would peck him again.

Mother Dubbins loved preparing for the

party for she had never been rich enough to have one before. You should have seen the table when it was ready! It simply groaned with good things!

Mother Dubbins sat at the top of the table, and who do you suppose sat at the bottom? Yes, you are quite right – Waddles the duck! She wore a new pink ribbon and looked very grand indeed.

"Three cheers for the duck!" cried everyone. "Hip-hip-hip-hurrah!"

"Quack, quack, quack, quack, it's really lovely to be back!" said the duck, and beamed at everyone.

Grandma's Doll

Grandma had a very old doll. She had had it when she was a little girl, and she had never given it away.

When Sophie went to see Grandma she always asked to see the old doll. Her name was Tabitha Jane.

She was a strange-looking doll, dressed in funny old-fashioned clothes. Her hair was very fuzzy and at the back it had come off a little and she was bald there.

She had bright blue eyes that didn't shut, and a round fat face made of china. She smiled and showed a set of white teeth. Her arms and legs wouldn't move very much, so she was rather a stiff sort of doll, and not very cuddlesome.

But there was one nice thing about her, and that was – she could say "Mamma, Mamma, Mamma". Sophie thought that was wonderful. It is true that Tabitha Jane wouldn't say "Mamma" unless you pulled a string in her back, but still she always spoke when you did that.

"You see, when I was small, little girls called their mothers 'Mamma' instead of 'Mummy', Sophie," said Grandma. "So that is why Tabitha Jane says 'Mamma' to me instead of 'Mummy'."

"Grandma, why didn't you ever give Tabitha Jane away?" asked Sophie. "You gave all your other toys away. I've got the rocking-horse you used to have. And Derek has all your bricks. But you have never given Tabitha Jane away. I wish you would give her to me. You don't want her now, do you?"

"Well, I feel I can't give Tabitha Jane away because she once did a very fine thing for me," said Grandma, and she looked rather mysterious. "She is a very special doll."

"What was the fine thing she did for you?" said Sophie, surprised.

"I can't tell you," said Grandma. "Nobody has ever believed it, so I never tell anyone now. I told lots of people when I was a little girl, but nobody believed me."

"I would believe you," said Sophie. "I would, really, Grandma. Please tell me."

"Listen. It's a very odd tale really, but it will help you to know why I have never given Tabitha Jane away.

"Once," went on Grandma, "when I was quite little, smaller than you, Sophie, I put Tabitha Jane to bed for the night.

She had a bed in the nursery, and I always used to undress her and put her to bed before I got undressed myself.

"I shared a bedroom with my little sister Mary. That night I popped Tabitha Jane down in her little bed, kissed her goodnight and left her. Very soon I was in my cot, and Mary, my little sister, was in hers. My mother, who was your great-grandmother, blew out our candle, and left us.

"Mary and I went to sleep. We slept until about midnight. Then I woke up. I could hear something."

"What could you hear?" said Sophie, looking at Grandma with wide-open eyes.

"I could hear a voice saying 'Mamma! Mamma! Mamma!'" said Grandma. "Yes, you may well look surprised, Sophie! I was surprised, too. I knew the voice of Tabitha Jane very well, and I felt sure it was my doll calling out 'Mamma! Mamma!' to me."

"What did you do?" said Sophie. "Oh, Grandma, this is wonderful. I love hearing this."

"Well, I sat up in bed and I listened.

And again I heard Tabitha Jane calling out. 'Mamma!' she called. 'Mamma!'

"So I jumped out of bed and ran into the nursery. It should have been dark there, but it wasn't – because part of the nursery was on fire!"

"Oh, Grandma – how dreadful!" cried Sophie.

"A hot coal had shot out of the fire and landed on the rug. It had set light to it, and the flames from the rug were burning the wooden chair standing there!" said Grandma. "The smell was awful.

"I stood at the door, full of horror, and all the time could hear that anxious little voice 'Mamma! Mamma! Mamma!'"

"Oh," said Sophie, "how wonderful of Tabitha Jane, Grandma! She warned you of the fire. Dear Tabitha Jane, I shall love her twice as much after this."

"Well, I was very frightened," said Grandma. "And I ran at once to my own mother's room, and I heard my voice too crying 'Mamma! Mamma! Mamma!' I woke my mother and father and they ran to the nursery, threw water on the flames and put out the fire."

"Oh, Grandma – what a lovely story!"

said Sophie. "Didn't your mother and father think Tabitha Jane was a marvellous doll?"

"They didn't believe me when I told them that Tabitha Jane had wakened me by calling 'Mamma'," said Grandma. "That made me very sad. They wouldn't even let me take her to bed at night, to reward her for being so good. I still had to leave her in her little bed in the nursery."

"Poor Tabitha Jane," said Sophie. "If you'll just lend her to me one night, Grandma, I'll cuddle her into bed with me. I'd love to. My mummy lets me have just one toy in bed."

Grandma pulled the string. Tabitha Jane at once said "Mamma". Sophie hugged the old doll.

"Grandma, I believe every word of your story. You can tell Tabitha Jane is a doll like that, just by looking at her darling face. Every time I come to see you, you must tell me the story of why you have never given Tabitha Jane away. You couldn't possibly give away a doll like that."

"Well," said Grandma, looking pleased, "if ever I do give her away, you shall have her, Sophie. I think you would love her as much as I did."

"And she might call *me* one night!" said Sophie. "Oh, I should like that!"

"Mamma," said Tabitha Jane, as Sophie pulled her string. "Mamma."

Wouldn't you love to hear her? She has such a dear little voice!

The Page That Blew Away

Old Dame Candy kept a fine little shop. It was a sweet-shop, and my goodness me, you should have seen the sweets she had in it!

It was no wonder the pixies and brownies pressed their noses against the window all day long, pointing to this and that.

"Oooh – butter-nut toffee," said one.

"And honey-balls," said another.

"And peppermint rock and raspberry drops and sugar-marbles!" said someone else. "How does Dame Candy think of all these lovely sweets?"

"She has a magic book," said Snoopy. "I've seen it."

"So have I," said Pry.

Both pixies nodded their heads. Yes – they had seen Dame Candy's book.

"Have you read it?" asked one of the brownies looking into the shop.

"Oh, no – we've only seen it from a distance," said Snoopy. "We live next door to Dame Candy, you know, and one day we put our heads out of the window and there she was, reading her magic sweet-book in the garden."

"We saw her making her sweets from the spells in her book," said Pry. "We did really."

"Piles of sugar-marbles, dozens of toffee-delights, hundreds of candy kisses," said Snoopy. "She just stirred something in a jug and muttered some magic words – then she tipped up the jug and out came lots of sweets. She poured them into a dish."

"And sold them in her shop next day," said Pry. "My, wouldn't I like to get hold of that book!"

They had never been able to do that because Dame Candy kept the book under the rug in her cat's basket. Her cat always slept there, night and day, and if she wasn't there, the dog got in to keep the basket warm. So Snoopy and Pry had never a chance to borrow the book.

But one day something unexpected happened. Pry saw Dame Candy sitting out at her garden table with her jug, dish and magic book. Aha! She was going to make a new batch of wonderful sweets. He called Snoopy.

"Look – she's making sweets again, using the spells in her magic book," whispered Pry. "If only she would leave her garden for a minute, we might be able to slip over the wall and have a look at the book."

"She'd turn us into toffee-balls if she saw us," said Snoopy. "And sell us too!"

"Yes – we won't do anything silly," said Pry, with a shiver.

They watched from the window. Dame Candy had already poured a heap of brown chocolates from her jug, and each chocolate had half a cherry on it. They did look nice.

And then one of the chocolates rolled off the table on to the grass. Dame Candy bent down to pick it up. At that very moment the wind blew hard – and a loose page in the magic book flew up into the air! It flew over the wall into Snoopy's garden, and settled down under a bush. Snoopy clutched Pry.

"Did you see?" he whispered. "A page flew out of the magic book – and it's in our garden!"

"Shh!" said Pry.

Dame Candy was coming to the wall. "Snoopy! Pry!" she called. "A page from my book has flown into your garden. Please get it for me."

"Come down and pretend to look everywhere," said Snoopy to Pry. "When you get a chance, put the page into your pocket. Then we'll say we can't find it and ask her in to look if she likes."

"Good! We'll read the page and make sweets all for ourselves!" said Pry. Down into the garden they went. Dame Candy had gone back to her seat. Pry put his head over the wall.

"We're just going to look for your page, Dame Candy," he called. "We'll hand it to you as soon as we've got it."

"Very well," said Dame Candy. "Look hard."

It didn't take Pry long to stuff the page into his pocket. Then Snoopy called over the wall.

"So sorry, Dame Candy, but we can't find the page anywhere. Would you like to come over and look?"

"No, thank you. I'm busy," said Dame Candy. "But let me warn you, Snoopy and Pry – if you keep the page yourself, and try to make sweets, I shall know it. Oh, yes, I shall know it!"

"We shouldn't dream of doing such a thing," said Snoopy, with a grin at Pry. The two went indoors, chuckling.

"That was easy as winking," said Pry. "Now let's see what the page is about."

They shut the windows and drew the curtains. They didn't want anyone

peeping in! Then they looked at the page out of Dame Candy's magic book.

"It's about peppermint rock," said Pry, in delight. "Our favourite sweet – would you believe it! Peppermint rock!"

"We'll make heaps and heaps," said Snoopy, rubbing his hands together. "What does the spell say?"

"We have to have a jug and a dish," said Pry, reading the page. "Well, we know that already. And we have to wear something blue to do this spell. Oh – so that's why old Dame Candy always wears a blue shawl round her! Have we anything blue to wear, Snoopy?"

"Our new blue caps!" said Snoopy, and they went to put them on.

"It's a very easy spell!" said Pry. "Look, we have to pour milk into the jug, stir with a poppyolly feather, drop in a lighted match, and then say 'Tirry-lirry-roona-moona-accra-rilly-POM!' And that's all."

"It seems very easy indeed," said Snoopy. "Is that really all?"

"Well, look at the page yourself," said Pry. So Snoopy looked. Yes, that was all.

They fetched a jug and a dish. They

poured milk into the jug. They got their poppyolly feather from the cupboard, and then they lit a match and dropped it into the jug. What a fizzle-fizzle, and what a strange green flame!

"Now for the magic word," said Pry, snatching up the page. "I'll say it – and you can pour out the peppermint rock, Snoopy. I hope our dish is big enough!"

He said the magic word loudly and clearly. "Tirry-lirry-roona-moona-accra-rilly-POM!"

And then Snoopy at once tipped up the jug and poured out. He looked greedily for sticks and sticks of peppermint rock – but all that came out was a stream of fine yellow powder!

"Pooh – what's this? This isn't peppermint!" said Pry, disappointed. "It's just powder. Something's gone wrong."

"I'm going to sneeze," said Snoopy, suddenly, and he sneezed very loudly indeed. "Whooosh-oo!"

He sneezed all over the dish, and the yellow powder flew up into the air at once. Pry felt a sneeze coming too. He threw back his head and sneezed violently.

"Whoooosh-oo, whooosh-oo, whooosh-oo!"

Then Snoopy joined in again, and soon both pixies were sneezing without stopping. The yellow powder flew all over the place, and the more it flew, the more they sneezed.

"What's happening?" gasped Pry, at last. "Oh, Snoopy – can this yellow powder be pepper? Have we made pepper instead of peppermint? Whooosh-oo!"

"We must have, whoosh-oo!" said Snoopy. "The spell's gone wrong."

There was a rap at the door. The pixies looked at one another, startled. "Who's there?" called Pry.

"Dame Candy," said a voice. "I've come for the page of my magic book. I told you I should soon know if you had it. I just waited to hear you sneeze – and you did!"

"Whooosh-oo!" sneezed Snoopy and Pry together.

The door opened and in came Dame Candy. She saw the page on the table and took it. The pixies went on sneezing miserably.

"You only had half the peppermint spell," said Dame Candy. "You have to read the bit on the next page in my book to complete the spell – then you'd have got a jugful of peppermint rock instead of pepper. Serves you right!"

She went out with the page of her magic book. Pry ran to the door.

"Take the pepper, please take it," he cried. "Whoosh-oo!"

"No, you can keep it," said Dame Candy,

with a laugh. "It's all over your kitchen by now – you won't get rid of it for days. That will teach you to take things that belong to someone else, Snoopy and Pry!"

It did – and it was a dreadful lesson to learn, because Snoopy and Pry didn't stop sneezing for nine days. And now, it's such a pity, they can't bear even to look at peppermint rock. That starts them sneezing again too! They'll be careful not to meddle with Dame Candy's spells again, won't they?

Puss!
Puss! Puss!

"Carolyn! Are you ready to take the things to Granny?" called her mother. "She said she wanted them before twelve o'clock, so you'd better go."

"I'll go now, Mummy," called back Carolyn, who was playing with the kitten. Her mother brought her the bag. It was full of things for the Christmas Fair which Granny was organising.

There was a pretty woollen shawl which Mother had knitted. There was a quilted tea cosy. There was a pair of mittens that Carolyn herself had knitted and embroidered. There were some egg-cosies and some babies' bootees.

"Granny will be very pleased to have all these things for her sale, won't she?" said Carolyn. "I'll just leave them here while I go and wash my hands, Mummy."

"Brush your hair, too," said her mother. "Granny likes to see you looking nice."

Carolyn left the kitten to play with its tail and ran upstairs. She soon came down again looking very clean and neat.

"You look nice," said her mother. "Give my love to Granny."

Carolyn kissed her goodbye and looked round to say goodbye to the kitten, too. But it wasn't there.

"Puss, puss, puss!" called Carolyn. "Come and say goodbye to me!"

But no kitten came. Carolyn called again. "Puss, puss, puss! Where are you, kitty?"

"It's asleep somewhere," said Mother. "Don't bother it. It will be ready to play with you when you come back to lunch. Hurry off now, darling."

"I did want to say goodbye to it," said Carolyn. "I do hope it hasn't run out into the road, Mummy."

"You'll see it if it has," said her mother. "I expect it's curled up in the armchair, fast asleep!"

Carolyn went off to Granny's. Granny was very pleased to see her, and took the bag from her at once. "You've just brought the things in time," she said. "I've got two of my helpers here, sorting out all the things for the stalls."

"Mummy's sent a nice lot of things," said Carolyn. "And I managed to finish the mittens for you, Granny! Shall I show them to you?"

"Not now, dear," said Granny. "I've got so much to do that I can't spare even a minute for my favourite little grand-daughter! I simply must get everything ready. Look, I have put out a bar of chocolate for you, and a ginger biscuit."

"Oh, thank you, Granny!" said Carolyn,

and went to get them. Granny always had some little treat for her.

"Goodbye, darling," said Granny. "I shall see you and Mummy this afternoon, shan't I? You're both coming to my little sale of work."

Carolyn ate the ginger biscuit, then ran all the way home with the bar of chocolate in her pocket. Mummy called to her as she came in. "Carolyn, did you see the kitten in the road anywhere? She's nowhere to be seen. I've called and called her, and hunted everywhere for the little thing."

"Oh dear!" said Carolyn. "Somebody's stolen her. Mummy, that's what must have happened. Somebody's stolen her! Oh dear!"

She burst into tears. The kitten was hers and she loved every bit of it from its absurd little tail to its little white whiskers. She began to hunt all over the house.

"Puss, puss, puss! Kitty, kitty, kitty! Where are you? Puss, puss, puss!"

But no kitten came darting out from under a bed, or round a corner. Carolyn hunted in the garden, looking under every bush. Still no kitten! She was very sad.

"Carolyn, come and have your lunch," called her mother. "I'm afraid the kitten has wandered away – but somebody may bring it back soon."

Poor Carolyn couldn't eat any lunch. She didn't want to go to Granny's Christmas Fair either.

"But you must go, dear," said her mother. "Granny will be so sad if you don't. She does want you to help with the teas."

Carolyn didn't want to disappoint Granny so she put on a clean dress and went off with her mother at three o'clock. Her eyes were still very red. She called the kitten once more.

"Puss, puss, puss, kitty, kitty! Do come, please do come."

"It won't," said her mother. "It isn't anywhere about, that's for certain, or it would be hungry by now and come crying for food."

That made Carolyn begin to cry all over again. She couldn't bear to think of a poor, hungry kitten!

When they arrived at the church hall a good many people were already there, buying all kinds of things from the stalls. Carolyn actually saw somebody buying the mittens she had made. How very proud she felt!

And then a very funny thing happened. As Carolyn was looking at a stall of books, one of the stall-keepers spoke to her. "You don't want to buy a kitten, I suppose, do you?"

Carolyn looked up in surprise. "No. I've got one. At least – I hope I have. It disappeared this morning and it hasn't come back yet. Why? Is there a kitten for sale today? Has someone given one? Oh, do let me see it. I love kittens."

"I've got it here, asleep in a box of jumble," said the stall-keeper, Mrs Jones. "It's sweet. Someone sent it along with other things in a basket this morning – fancy that! Your granny told me to put the kitten on my stall, but nobody seems to want to buy it."

She went to a box behind her stall, and Carolyn followed her. There, lying fast asleep, was the prettiest little white kitten you ever saw. Carolyn gazed at it, and then she gave such a loud cry that everyone jumped.

"But – that's my kitten! My very own white kitten! Kitty, kitty!"

The kitten woke up and stretched itself.

It looked at Carolyn, gave a delighted mew, and leaped straight on to her shoulder. It rubbed its little white head against her cheek and purred.

"Mummy! Mummy! Look, I've found my kitten!" shouted Carolyn. "Look, do look. It's here, safe and sound. But how did it get here? Granny, who brought it?"

"Now let me see – it was asleep in one of the bags of goods brought this morning," said Granny. "Dear me, which one was it now? Oh, yes – this one. Does anyone know whose this bag is?"

Carolyn looked at it and gave a squeal. "It's Mummy's! It's the one I brought this morning, full of things for your sale, Granny."

"Well – you brought the kitten in it too, then," said Granny. "It was asleep under a woolly shawl. Oh Carolyn, what a thing to do!"

Everyone began to laugh. Carolyn laughed too, very red in the face. Oh dear, oh dear – to think she had upset herself all day long because her kitten

had gone – and she had carried it all the way to Granny's in Mummy's shopping bag. Well, well – there's no knowing what some people will do!

The kitten was a great success at the Christmas Fair. When children came to buy, what do you think Carolyn did? She charged any boy or girl ten pence to play for five minutes with the kitten – what fun everybody had!

She had seventy pence to give to Granny at the end of the sale. Granny smiled and stroked the kitten's head. Then she gave Carolyn a pretty blue ribbon.

"A reward for a good little kitten!" she said. Wasn't it nice of her?

Someone Likes the Mud

Neil and Helen were to go for a picnic if it was fine. Mother said she would take them on Saturday, and they would go to Cuckoo Wood and have a lovely time.

And then it began to rain, just on the Friday evening! The children were so disappointed.

"Shan't we be able to go, Mummy?" asked Neil.

"Not if it doesn't stop raining," said their mother. "The woods will be too wet and muddy."

All night it rained, and then it stopped the next day about ten o'clock. "Oh, do let's go, Mummy!" cried Helen.

But Mother shook her head. "Look at the muddy paths. It wouldn't be any pleasure to go picnicking today."

"It's too bad!" Neil cried angrily.

"Horrid mud! Nasty mud! Spoiling our picnic! Nobody likes the mud, nobody at all. I don't know why we have it!"

"You're wrong, Neil; someone does like the mud," said his mother.

"Well, I don't know who, then!" said Neil sulkily. "Children don't. Grown-ups don't. The cat doesn't. I shouldn't think any animal does – nasty, wet, sticky stuff!"

His mother laughed. "Come out into the garden with me," she said. "I'll spread a waterproof sheet on the garden seat and we'll sit there to watch someone who loves the mud!"

The children were surprised. Who was going to come into their garden and like the mud?

They followed their mother into the garden. She spread a big waterproof sheet on the damp seat and they all sat down in

the warm sun. Mother looked up into the air. "What a lot of birds there are, flying high up!" she said.

"What are they? Are they larks?" asked Neil.

"No," said his mother. "Some are swifts – those sooty black ones that look like flying anchors in the sky. But most are the pretty steel-blue swallows, and their cousins the house-martins. Very soon they will fly down to our garden and you will see them closely."

"But why will they fly down?" asked Helen in surprise.

"Because they like that nice muddy patch over there!" said Mother. "The weather has been so hot and dry, and there has been no mud anywhere at all. But today there is plenty, and the swallows and martins are happy."

As she spoke, some of the little long-tailed birds flew down, twittering loudly. They went to the muddy patch that Mother had spoken of, and began to scrape up some of the mud in their beaks. The children were very surprised.

"Are they eating it?" asked Neil.

"Are they going to make mud-pies?" asked Helen.

Mother laughed. "No! Watch where they take the mud. Look! that swallow has flown into the old shed – and that martin has flown up to where the roof comes out over your bedroom window, Helen. They are going to make their nests of the mud! They are so pleased to find some today!"

The children were thrilled. When Mother went indoors, they still stayed in the garden, watching. They went into the old shed and saw that the swallow was building a saucer of mud on a beam that ran across the top of the roof.

"Isn't it clever?" said Neil. "It's making a real, proper nest of mud. When it dries it will be hard and safe. Now let's watch the martins."

The martins were even cleverer. They had stuck pellets of mud against the wall over the bedroom, and they kept flying down to the muddy patch for more and more beakfuls of mud. Soon the children could quite well see how the nest would be made.

"Just stuck against the wall with mud!"

said Neil. "Well, I should never have thought of making a nest like that!"

It was so interesting to watch the birds at work in the mud that the children forgot all about their disappointment. Mother was pleased with them. "We'll go picnicking tomorrow," she said. "It's going to be very hot again. We shall enjoy the woods – and you've really been very good about your disappointment."

"Well, you were quite right, Mummy!"

said Neil. "Someone does like the mud, and it'll be fun when they lay their eggs and we see the young ones peeping out of these strange nests!"

Would you like to see the birds working in the mud? Well, when there is a hot, dry spell, and all the puddles are dried up, water a patch in your garden and make some mud. Then watch for the excited swallows and martins to find it and use it for their strange little nests!

Old
Mister Surly

Robert Brown sat on his front doorstep and wondered how to get a job. It would have to be on Saturdays because he went to school the other days – or it would have to be before or after school.

"Dad can't get any work – and Mother's ill, and we are such a large family," said Robert to himself, thinking of his five brother and sisters. "If I could just get even a pound a day it would help."

He set off to look for a little job of work to do. But he was very small for his age and nobody would try him.

"No!" said the man at the newspaper shop, "I don't want a baby like you! You'd never be able to deliver my newspapers for me! You'd fall off the bike!"

"No!" said the chemist. "You won't do for me! I want a much older boy!"

"No!" said old Mrs Smith, when he went to ask if he could weed her garden each week. "I want a gardener to do that, not a little rascal like you!"

So it didn't seem a bit of good trying to get any work to do. Robert sat down on his front doorstep again and felt very unhappy. Then he heard the clump-clump of heavy feet and he looked up to see who was coming.

It was old Mister Surly, who lived at the corner house all alone. People said he had a lot of money, but he didn't look like it, for his clothes were dusty and dirty, his boots were never cleaned, and his hat had a hole it it. He wore thick glasses, and was so bad-tempered that boys and girls always ran away when they saw him.

Just as he came up to Robert he gave a groan and stopped. He leaned against the wall and Robert saw that he was very pale. "He's ill!" thought the little boy and jumped up, for he was a kind little fellow.

"Is anything the matter?" he asked Mister Surly. "Can I help you?"

"My eyes have gone wrong," said Mister Surly. "I can't see. I feel ill.

Will you guide me home?"

So Robert took his arm and guided him down the street to the little house where Mister Surly lived. He took him right up to the door and then unlocked it with the key Mister Surly gave him, for the old man could not see the lock. He went indoors with him, and looked round. My, what an untidy house! Newspapers thrown everywhere, dirty dishes on the table and in the sink, and everything covered with dust! Robert thought of his own nice clean home and turned up his nose. Fancy living in a place like this!

"Thanks, my boy," said old Mister Surly, and sat down on a dusty chair. "That's the first time anyone has ever shown a kindness to me! Now you run off, or your mother will be wondering where you are."

Robert said goodbye and ran off. He kept thinking of the old fellow all that day, and wondering how he was getting on all alone in his untidy house.

"I suppose his eyes are so bad that he can't see how dirty and dusty it is," thought Robert. "It must be horrid to be old and live all alone. He must be very lonely."

The next morning, before school, the little boy slipped up to Mister Surly's house. He knocked on the door and a voice said, "Come in! The door isn't locked."

He went in. Mister Surly was sitting in a chair, looking ill. There was no fire. Robert thought it all looked very horrid and uncomfortable.

"How are you today, sir?" he asked.

"Bad, my boy, bad!" said Mister Surly, with a groan. "So cold, too!"

"I'll light your fire, sir!" said Robert

eagerly. "You'll be warmer then!"

He lit the gas fire for the old man. Then he cleared up the newspapers and put the room tidy. "Would you like me to get you anything to eat, sir?" he asked. "I can cook bacon and eggs. I do at home sometimes when there's any to cook."

"Thanks, thanks," said Mister Surly. So Robert hunted about and found some bacon and an egg and a frying pan. Then a fine smell rose in the air as the bacon cooked in the pan. Robert soon took a tray to the old man and asked him if he should put on a kettle and make him some tea or coffee.

"Then I'm afraid I must go," he said, "or I'll be late for school. But I'll come in tonight, if you like, and see if there is anything I can do. Shall I tell my mother to ask someone to come in and clean up a bit for you?"

"No, thanks," said Mister Surly, with a frown. "I don't want any woman messing round my things. You come in tonight Robert. I don't mind you."

The boy ran off and was just in time for school. He thought about Mister Surly as he worked, and wondered what the old man was doing, all alone, with no one to speak to him or look after him.

"Well, as I can't seem to get a job of work, I might as well do something for nothing, and see what I can do for Mister Surly," he thought. So that night he went round to the old man again, and found Mister Surly eagerly waiting for him.

"I've got sausages and tomatoes," said Mister Surly. "Can you cook them? If you can, take four sausages for yourself, and three tomatoes, and we'll have a fine supper together."

Well, Robert was very hungry, and

soon the two were eating a most delicious meal. Then Robert made the old man's bed. After that he went to the sink and washed up every dirty dish and cup he could see! He swept up the room, tidied it, and put a kettle on so that Mister Surly could make himself a hot drink later on. He gave the newspaper to the old man – but Mister Surly didn't seem to want to read it. Instead he asked Robert to talk to him and tell him about himself.

So Robert told him about his father who couldn't get any work, and his mother, who was ill, and his five brothers and sisters. He told him how hard he had tried to get a job of work to do so that he might earn some money to buy something for his mother. "And I couldn't get any work at all," said Robert, with a sigh.

"Well, you are doing plenty for me," said the old man. "I wonder why you are doing all this, Robert."

"Oh," said Robert, "you were looking ill, and I was sorry for you – especially when I saw the muddle your house was in."

"You just did it out of kindness, then?" said Mister Surly. "Did you hope I would pay you?"

"Oh, no," said Robert at once. "Of course not. Besides I'm sure you haven't much money to spare, because you go about in such dusty old clothes and you have a hole in your hat."

"Good gracious me, am I as bad as that?" said Mister Surly. "I must really look into this. Will you come shopping with me when I am better, and help me to choose some new clothes and a new hat?"

Well, Robert promised that he would – and in two days' time the old man was about again. He and Robert went into the next town on the bus, and, my goodness, what fine clothes Mister Surly bought for himself – and a very beautiful hat too, brown, with a dark-brown ribbon round it.

"And now, what about you?" he suddenly said to Robert. "You look a bit as if you could do with some new clothes too. Come along!"

And will you believe it, he bought Robert a new suit, a new cap, a new tie, and even new boots! Then he took him

into a shop, and bought him the biggest strawberry ice they had! Robert could hardly believe his eyes.

"And now we'll buy a present for your mother, and for each of your brothers and sisters," said Mister Surly. So off they went, and bought a red jumper for Robert's mother, big dolls for his sisters, and railway trains for his brothers. Then the old man bought a great bag of currant buns, and off they went home.

What a surprise for Robert's family! His mother stared in astonishment and all his brothers and sisters shouted for joy to see their presents.

"But I don't understand," said Robert's mother. "Why do you do all this for us?"

"Well," said Mister Surly, "this small boy of yours came and looked after me – tidied my house – cooked meals for me – washed up – swept the floor – made my bed – all out of kindness, not expecting a single penny, and never asking for one though he badly needed the money. He didn't know I was rich! But I am, although I live in such a little house and don't have anyone to see me. So I planned a little surprise to pay

back Robert's kindness – and I have found work for his father, so please tell him to go to his new job tomorrow."

Well! Would you believe it? Everyone stared in delight. To think that old Mister Surly, whom nobody liked, should do all this!

"And will you let Robert come in and do a few things for me still?" asked the old man. "I will pay him this time – five pounds a week!"

Robert nearly fell off his chair in surprise and delight. "But I don't want to be paid!" he cried. "I'll come because I like you!"

"That's the nicest thing that has ever been said to me!" said Mister Surly, and he went red with pleasure. "No, Robert – you have done a lot for nothing – now you shall get a job of work with me, and be paid. You are worth every penny!"

So now Robert has his job of work – and very much he enjoys it too, especially when he shares sausages and tomatoes with Mister Surly. His father has a job as well – and everyone is happy.

"You're a good boy, Robert!" his mother

sometimes says to him. "If you hadn't been kind to an old man that day, we wouldn't have had all this good luck!"

As for old Mister Surly – well, you wouldn't know him now, he is so smart and neat, and you should see his face! It is all smiles and beams, with never a frown to be seen!

The Witch-Sixpence

Once upon a time Skippetty-Hop the pixie got into trouble. He had a patch of ground up on the hill that he was supposed to grow vegetables on, but he just didn't bother about it, and it grew nothing but weeds. The seeds of these weeds blew on to other people's ground, and they were very angry about it.

"What is the use of us keeping our ground well-dug and weeded and hoed if Skippetty-Hop lets weeds grow all over his patch!" they cried. "His horrid weeds send seeds on to our patches, and we have twice the work to do. It is time that Skippetty-Hop was scolded for it."

So Gobo the pixie, Tickles the brownie, and Hallo the elf marched to Skippetty-Hop's and gave him a great scolding.

"We shall give you a good spanking if

you don't weed your patch and dig it up well," said Gobo.

"We shall spank you each day till you do as you're told," said Tickles.

"In fact, I feel like beginning the spanking now," said Hallo.

"No, no, please don't," said Skippetty-Hop, alarmed. "I'll go straightaway and weed my patch."

He put on his hat and went up the hill. It was a hot day. Skippetty-Hop began to pull up the weeds. There were dandelions and thistles, daisies and plantains, and they all seemed to have very big roots. Poor Skippetty-Hop! He soon grew very hot and tired. When he had pulled up all

the weeds he put them into his barrow to wheel away. He looked at his patch of ground.

"Oh dear, now I've got to dig that all up!" he said, "I really can't! I shall ask someone to do it for me, and I will pay them for it."

So he went to Getaway the elf and asked him if he would dig up the ground for him for sixpence. But Getaway laughed and said no, he would charge much more than sixpence! Then Skippetty-Hop went to Jolly the pixie, and asked him. But Jolly said no, he wasn't going to do hard work like that for sixpence. And Pitapat said the same. So Skippetty-Hop scratched his head and wondered what to do.

And then an idea came into his lazy little head. He had a witch-sixpence. He would hide it somewhere in his patch and he would put up a notice saying: "Lost in this patch, a fine sixpence. Anyone finding it may keep it!"

Then every one would come along and dig in his patch of ground for the sixpence, and they wouldn't find it because it was a witch-sixpence, and nobody could see a witch-sixpence when it was on the ground! Witch-sixpences can only be seen in the hand. Ha, ha! Skippetty-Hop would have his patch of ground dug up nicely, and nobody would find the sixpence; so he would have his digging done for nothing!

Well, Skippetty-Hop put up the notice, and everyone came to look at it. Nobody knew that the sixpence was a witch one. They thought it was an ordinary sixpence. They all read the notice and rubbed their hands in glee.

"I'm going to find that sixpence!" said Sandy Rabbit, who was good at digging.

"I'm going to have a try too," said Mowdie Mole.

"So am I," said Getaway the elf. Jolly and Pitapat turned up too, to look for that sixpence. So did Dame Skinny and Mister Highhat, who both liked to get something for nothing. What a to-do there was in Skippetty-Hop's patch! You should have seen them. Sandy Rabbit scraped away hard. Mowdie Mole ran tunnels here and there. Getaway dug with his spade. Jolly turned up the ground with his fork. Pitapat used his new trowel. Dame

Skinny turned up the earth with a hoe. Mister Highhat used his hands. Everyone was as busy as could be.

But nobody found that sixpence! Each one of them touched it, but as it could not be seen on the ground no one found it! Skippetty-Hop grinned to himself as he watched them all. This was fun!

When the sun set everyone stood up, hot and tired. They saw Skippetty-Hop grinning, and Getaway wondered why.

"Is that sixpence really there?" he said. "If it isn't, you'll get into trouble!"

Skippetty-Hop stopped grinning. "Dear me, Getaway, of course the sixpence is there!" he said. "There's no need for anyone to look for it if they don't want to. In fact, I think you'd all better go home. Goodnight!"

Now, as everyone went home, they met Gobo, Tickles and Hallo going up to Skippetty-Hop's patch to see if he had done as they said and weeded and dug his patch. And Getaway told them how everyone had worked hard to find a lost sixpence and hadn't found it!

"That's a witch-sixpence Skippetty-Hop

has hidden there, sure as anything!" said Hallo as he went up the hill. "It's a trick of his to make them dig up his ground for him, the lazy little creature!"

They went to where Skippetty-Hop was standing looking at his nicely-turned up patch of ground. He was saying the spell that would show him where the witch-sixpence was. He suddenly saw it shining there, and picked it up at once.

"So that was a witch-sixpence you made everyone hunt for!" said Hallo. "If you would use some of your brains for work, you would get on well! You are a

lazy, cunning little pixie. We shall tell every one that it was a witch-sixpence you made them hunt for – and I wonder what they will say to that."

"No, please, don't tell them," begged Skippetty-Hop, going quite pale with fright. "They will all come up and spank me."

"That's just what you deserve!" said Tickles. "Well, you may choose, Skippetty-Hop. You can come to my patch tomorrow and dig it over well for me; and go to Hallo's the next day and dig his; and to Gobo's the next day and dig his; or we will tell every one about the trick you played on them!"

"I shall have to come and dig over your patches," said Skippetty-Hop sulkily. "I can't have you telling people about my witch-sixpence. But I wish now that I had dug my own patch myself, for it seems I have to dig three patches instead of one!"

"It serves you right," said Tickles. "You have been just a bit too clever, Skippetty-Hop."

So now Skippetty-Hop is busy digging up Hallo's patch for him, and after that is done he has the other two to do, and he is getting just as hot and tired as Sandy Rabbit got, and Mowdie Mole, and all the rest!

I don't think he will use that witch-sixpence again in a hurry, do you?

Butterfingers

There was once an old woman called Dame Hopscotch, who kept a butter shop. Her butter was lovely. It was a deep, rich yellow, and nobody ever wanted jam on their bread when it was spread with Dame Hopscotch's butter.

She stored her butter in a cool, dark shed, and kept the key of the shed tied on to her belt. She was always afraid of robbers, and many a rogue had tried to steal her butter and carry away a big barrel of it.

One day her little servant Pop-Out came running in to Dame Hopscotch, in a great state.

"Someone's been at the butter!" he said. "Look at this barrel!"

Dame Hopscotch looked.

"Dear me!" she said, "it's been all

messed about by someone digging in it with his hands. What a shame! Now that barrel is spoilt. I wonder who the thief is."

"It might be Pinkity, and it might be Tootle, and it might be Tiptoe," said Pop-Out. "And it might be Twinkle, or Skippetty or..."

"Yes, it might," said Dame Hopscotch. "They've all be playing round this shed. Now I wonder which of those mischievous pixies it is!"

She thought for a little while, then she rubbed her hands in glee and turned to Pop-Out.

"Pop out and fetch me a rubber ball from the toyshop," she said. "I have a plan to find the thief."

Off went Pop-Out, and soon came back with a small, round ball.

"Thank you," said Dame Hopscotch. "Now put a nice fresh barrel in the same place as you found the spoilt one, Pop-Out."

Pop-Out did as he was told, and the little pixies playing nearby came to watch him rolling the barrel into the big shed.

"Ooh, butter, butter!" they cried. "Give

us some, Pop-Out. We do love butter!"

Pop-Out shook his head. He locked the shed door behind him and ran back to the house to give Dame Hopscotch the key. She took it and tied it on her belt.

Soon the sun went down and darkness fell. Dame Hopscotch took a lantern and went out to look at her shed. She went carefully all round it and at last found a little hole, not much bigger than a pixie's fist, in one side.

"Ha!" she said. "That's where the rascal got my butter! He put in his hand, took off the lid of the barrel, and then dug out handfuls of my beautiful butter! I'll catch him tomorrow, as sure as eggs are eggs and butter is butter!"

The next day Dame Hopscotch stood at her window and looked out. About a dozen pixies were playing round about her shed. When the morning was nearly gone the old woman sent Pop-Out to the shed with the key.

"Pop out and see if any more butter is gone," she said. Soon Pop-Out came back, shaking his head dolefully.

"That new barrel is all spoilt!" he said. "One of those wicked little pixies has taken the butter again. I wish I knew which one it was!"

"You'll soon see!" Dame Hopscotch said, and she picked up her bunchy skirts and went over to where the pixies were playing twos and threes.

"Come here!" called Dame Hopscotch, and they all ran round her. "Here is a fine ball," said the old woman. "Stand round me in a ring and catch it in turn. The one that catches it every time shall have a bag of sweeties."

"Ooh!" cried the pixies in joy and jumped up and down excitedly. They stood round Dame Hopscotch and she threw the ball to each one in turn. They all caught it beautifully except one little pixie who dropped it. Round and round went the ball, and every single time the same pixie dropped it on the ground.

"You are a baby!" cried the others. "Whatever is the matter with you,

Skippetty? You caught our ball the other day!" Skippetty blushed red.

Dame Hopscotch looked at him sternly. "I can tell you why Skippetty keeps dropping the ball," she said. "Show us your hands, Skippetty."

Skippetty held out his hands. They were all slippery with butter!

"Look!" said Dame Hopscotch. "He has been robbing my butter barrels, digging into them with his hands! That is why he couldn't catch the ball, but dropped it every time! His hands were too slippery to hold it!"

And do you know, ever since that day we call out "Butterfingers" to anyone who misses catching a ball!

I Don't Know How to Dance!

"Linda, I've arranged for you to go to dancing classes," her mother said, one day. "You'll like that."

"But I don't know how to dance!" said Linda, looking scared. "I really don't."

"Well, you'll learn," said James, her brother. "You'll have to waltz and polka and foxtrot, and..."

"I don't know how to," said Linda. "I shall never be able to do those. I don't want to go."

"And you'll have to do the Highland fling and the sailor's hornpipe," said her big sister, Laura.

Linda was really frightened. How difficult all this sounded! "But I don't know how to dance," she said. "And I don't want to, either. I'm not going."

"Linda!" said her mother, in surprise.

"Don't be silly. Laura will take you this afternoon and leave you at the door. You will have to take you dancing shoes with you – they are the ones you wear for a party."

Linda was miserable. How could she dance when she didn't know how to? All the other boys and girls would be able to and she would have to stand alone and feel a baby. She wouldn't go!

Laura set out with her that afternoon. Linda had her shoes in a bag. But when they got to the end of the road, Linda slipped away from Laura! Laura had met a friend and was talking to her. It was easy for Linda to run away without being seen. She raced down the road and round the corner and round another corner. Then she heard the sound of jolly music being played and she stopped. She was very fond of music.

The music was coming from an open door. Two children passed Linda and ran in, laughing. Linda stole up to the door and looked in. There was a room inside with a shiny wooden floor. Little chairs were set round the walls and children

were sitting on them chattering. The music came from a cassette player in the corner – tumpty-tumpty-tum-tum, tippitty-tippitty-tip!

"Fairies!" suddenly cried a voice, and a smiling lady came into the room. "This is fairy music! Who will be the fairies for me this afternoon?"

"I will, I will!" cried the children, and they rushed on to the floor. They flapped their arms as if they were wings and ran about on tiptoe, keeping time to the music.

Linda watched. What a lovely game! She could easily play that! Then the music changed and became a march.

"Wooden soldiers!" cried the lady. "Who

will be wooden soldiers? Make a line, please, and march – left, right, left, right – that's right, wooden soldiers. Now play your drums – boom-boom-boom!"

And all the children played pretend drums, and shouted "Boom-boom-boom!" Linda wished she could do that, too.

Then the smiling lady saw her peeping and came over to her. "Well, dear?" she said. "What's your name?"

"Linda," said Linda, shyly.

"Oh, so you're Linda!" said the lady,

and took her by the hand. "Come along then and be a soldier – you can march with Edwin, he's a fine soldier!"

So Linda marched and beat a pretend drum and shouted "Boom-boom-boom!" like the others. Then the music changed again and this time they had to be trees waving in the wind, saying "Sh-sh-sh-sh" all the time. Linda really did feel as if she was a tree, and it felt nice.

She was very sorry when it was all over. "Come next Thursday," said the smiling lady. "Don't forget."

"Oh, I won't!" said Linda, pleased. And then, dear me, she wondered whatever Mother and Laura would say to her when she went home and told them she had run away because she wouldn't go to the dancing class and dance the Highland fling and waltz and polka and do the foxtrot.

Suddenly, she saw Laura peeping in at the door, smiling. She ran to her. "Laura! How did you know I was here? I've had a lovely time."

"Well, I guessed you'd go to the dancing class by yourself," said Laura. "Though you shouldn't have run away like that. I've come to fetch you home."

"But I didn't go to the dancing class, I came here," said Linda. "I don't know how to dance and I don't want to learn. I want to come here and play like we did this afternoon."

"Well, you can, silly!" said Laura. "This is the dancing class!"

What a surprise for Linda! She hasn't got over it yet!